D1604312

Come To Laugh

African Traditional Theatre in Ghana

Kwabena N. Bame

LILIAN BARBER PRESS, INC.
New York

First published in the United States of America 1985 by

LILIAN BARBER PRESS, INC.
Box 232
New York, NY 10163

An earlier edition of part one of this book was published in Accra by
Baafour Educational Enterprises Limited (Publishing Division) who have
kindly given permission for the publication of this revised edition. Part
two of this work has never been previously published.

Library of Congress Cataloging in Publication Data

Bame, Kwabena N.
    Come to laugh.

    Bibliography: p.
        1. Theater – Ghana.   2. Folk-drama – Ghana – History and criticism.
    3. Comedians – Ghana.   4. Ghana – Popular culture.   I. Title.
    PN2990.4.B35 1984   792'.09667   84-6259
    ISBN 0-936508-07-8
    ISBN 0-936508-08-6 (pbk.)   75990

Photo credit: The publishers wish to acknowledge their gratitude to Mr. K.
Andoh, Staff photographer of the Institute of African Studies, University
of Ghana, Legon, for the photographs that appear in this book.

CONTENTS

PART I

PART II

Preface

African social and ceremonial activities are replete with differing forms of drama. There is an element of drama in all the various African festivals, funeral celebrations, ceremonial occasions, social singing, dancing, and storytelling activities. This book is a study of one type of African drama as it is performed in the Republic of Ghana.

The plays, which I term in this book comic plays, are staged by concert parties – an intriguing name for itinerant theatre troupes in Ghana. They may quite rightly be regarded as a development of the habit of dramatization and a focus for laughter which Ghanaians share with other Africans and indeed with other peoples of the world. Comic plays provide one of the commonest forms of entertainment in Ghana today.

Although concert parties have been performing in Ghana for well over fifty years, their plays have become a more lucrative business of late than they once were. The number of persons seeking either a full- or part-time work means of earning their living in this way has increased remarkably. The analysis of the plays in this book throws light on why the plays have gained such popularity. In order to place the plays in a proper setting – and by so doing, I hope, make the analysis more meaningful – I have had briefly to trace the history and describe the various elements of the plays before dealing with their social functions.

I would like to thank Professor J. H. Kwabena Nketia, sometime Director of the Institute of African Studies, University of Ghana, Legon, for the encouragement he gave me when I showed him my first short draft of this study. His continued encouragement and interest have been of great help to me. My deepest gratitude and appreciation go to Miss Marjorie E. Nockolds, my former English teacher and friend, and to Professor R. D. Greenfield, my former

5

colleague at Legon and onetime Dean of the Faculty of Arts and Social Sciences, University of Benin, Nigeria, who have been overwhelmingly kind in separately carrying out a careful scrutiny of this book and in making invaluable suggestions. It also gives me pleasure to acknowledge my indebtedness to Professor John Povey of the African Studies Center, University of California, Los Angeles, for making useful suggestions for the improvement of the manuscript.

Many thanks are also due to other friends and scholars who have read the manuscript and made useful suggestions to me. I am indebted to Messrs. Emmanuel Siaw and B. M. Tetteh of the Institute of African Studies, Legon, who did most of the typing of the manuscript at its various stages. Finally, I wish to render my special thanks to the numerous concert parties whose performances have made possible the writing of this book.

K.N.B.

PART I
African Traditional Theatre in Ghana

1
The History of The Concert Parties

The Beginnings

By many standards, concert parties in Ghana are a relatively recent form of dramatic entertainment yet they draw on deep indigenous roots as well as foreign influences.[1] Elements of their present form can be traced back more than sixty years to the "concerts" given by Teacher Yalley in Sekondi, a seaport in what is now the Western Region of Ghana. Yalley was the headmaster of a Sekondi elementary school who began to act in his school's "Empire Day" concerts in 1918. His performances interwove jokes, singing, and dancing, and he wore fancy dress, wigs, false moustaches and the white makeup of a minstrel. The shows were performed in English and tickets were expensive, with the result that most of the audience were from the educated Ghanaian elite. According to people who saw these shows, Yalley's sketches were assisted by a tap dancer and a harmonium player who together provided a program of then-current popular Western dance music, such as Black American ragtime and ballroom dances like the foxtrot, quickstep and waltz. Bob Johnson, the famous Fanti comedian, who was a boy then, recalled in later life that Yalley's shows lasted three hours.[2]

Three features of Yalley's concerts are of significance – the elite character of his audience, which the use of English in the performances and the very high ticket prices helped to maintain;[3] other significant non-African influences; and the importance of music in the evening's entertainment. Apocalyptic interpretations of the influence of Western culture on Africa sometimes give an impression of pervasive and relentless Westernization. Yet the history of concert parties in Ghana belies this. As with the development of "highlife" and other forms of popular music in Ghana,[4] which ran parallel with and has been intimately connected with the develop-

8

ment of concert parties, the concert-party form can be seen to have shrugged off its elitist origins, at first gradually and then with accelerating momentum. It fast incorporated vernacular elements in language, theme and form, while retaining buried though recognizable aspects of non-African influence.

The career of Ishmael Johnson, the most influential of the pioneer concert-party leaders illustrates some aspects of this development. Born in about 1904 in the coastal town of Saltpond, Johnson soon moved to Sekondi. As a young man in elementary school in the 1920s,[5] Johnson took part in "concerts" organized by his school and was impressed by the performances of Teacher Yalley. He certainly also helped in some of the menial tasks involved in putting on Yalley's concerts, and may even have appeared on stage with Yalley. Johnson was also impressed by church-organized musical morality plays – the "cantatas" – often performed in the vernacular, and silent films, including those featuring Charlie Chaplin, whose characteristic walk Johnson imitated. Some time in the 1920s he formed a group with two schoolfriends, C.B. Hutton and J.B. Ansah which performed in school holidays and at weekends as far away as the coastal town of Axim, forty-seven miles west of Sekondi. Johnson's group, which became known as The Versatile Eight and so probably augmented its core of three players, clearly aimed its performances at a wider audience than did Yalley. Its entrance fee was sixpence and sometimes threepence. Other influences besides Yalley, the cantatas and silent films were apparent in the group's performances. Johnson recalls that "Ansah played the role of Gentleman, Hutton was his Wife and I was the Houseboy."[6]

The gentleman, the female impersonator and the servant or "houseboy," better known as "the joker" or – after Bob Johnson, the "Original Bob" – as the "Bob" have remained central characters in concert-party performances. They are perhaps best seen as the result of a convergence of influences. Johnson has told of the influence of the Black American vaudevillians, Glass and Grant, who resided in Accra between 1924 and 1926 and toured widely performing for elite audiences. Their act featured joking, tap-dancing – an element still found in concert party performances – and the singing of ragtime, with Glass playing the "minstrel" and Grant, the female impersonator, as his wife. Williams and Marbell, a Ghanaian duo, took over this format when Glass and Grant left, also for elite audiences.[7] Another foreign influence on

9

Johnson – which, if its parallel impact on popular music is any in-dication,[8] was rapidly indigenized – came from seamen who frequented the Optimism Club near his home in Sekondi. Liberian seamen sang "sea-shanties and highlifes to the accompaniment of guitar and musical saw," and Black Americans performed "comedy sketches and [sang] foxtrots and ragtimes." It was Black American sailors, too, who gave Johnson the nickname "Bob."[9]

In addition to such non-African influences, Johnson recalls the importance of indigenous cultural forms, notably the *Anansesem* storytelling tradition which featured the mischievous *Ananse*, the spider – a likely prototype of or major contribution to the concert-party joker, the "Bob." In *Anansesem*, the teller dramatizes his performances with different voices and sometimes dresses up as well. The complexity of the roots of concert-party styles – and even Black American influences might, of course, contain *re-imported* features originally taken from Africa to North America by slaves – is apparent from the fact that *Anansesem* sometimes made use of female impersonation. Johnson, for example, recalls from his boyhood a male teller of *Anansesem* who "sometimes played the role of an old woman. He wore women's clothes, a cloth and cover-shoulder, and he had a big bustle which wobbled as he walked along on a stick just like an old woman."[10] The *Anansesem* are also stories with implicit or explicit moral lessons, a central feature of the plays of the concert parties in their modern, fully indigenized form.

After completing elementary education, Bob Johnson had to decide whether or not to brave the hazards of a career in comic acting or to opt for the security and relative comfort of a white-collar job. He decided to take the risk and in 1930 formed a new professional concert party with his friends Ansah and Hutton. This concert trio was called The Two Bobs – the "Bobs" being Johnson and Ansah – and the female impersonator, Hutton, who in 1932 began being billed as "the Carolina Girl." Another group, The Axim Trio, was formed in the early 1930s, but it was The Two Bobs which gained a particularly strong reputation because of its widespread touring, reaching a wider audience than had Teacher Yalley or Williams and Marbell. The shows, as Collins describes, were[11]

> publicized by a masked bell-ringer wearing a billboard, and they commenced with a half-hour in-

Kwaa Mensah's concert party in the fifties. Guitarist Kwaa is
in drag and the "Bob" is on the right, wearing minstrel make-up.

troduction consisting of an "Opening Chorus" of quick-
steps, danced and sung by the three comedians, followed by an "In," during which one of the Bobs sang
ragtimes, and closing with a "Duet" of joking by the two
Bobs. Music was supplied by the group's trap drum-
mer, who was usually helped by members of a school
orchestra hired for the night. The play proper, or
"Scene," that followed the introduciton lasted an hour

and was performed in English, with an occasional translation into Akan; this concert audience was less educated than its high-class counterpart. Yet another difference between the two varieties of concert was that Johnson incorporated, in addition to popular Western songs, a few highlifes sung in pidgin English.

This account perhaps underestimates the degree of indigenous content, particularly the use of the vernacular,[12] although the vernacular content may well have varied to suit a particular audience.

In 1935 Johnson left The Two Bobs and joined two members of a concert party called The Axim Trio which had been formed soon after The Two Bobs. This "trio" in fact involved more than three people and the term "trio" in the names of concert parties has generally not been restricted to groups of three persons. Perhaps the original trio was argued to be the archetypal group and the term has thus been retained as an emotive and expected part of a group's title. The reason for the break-up of The Two Bobs was that in 1937 a Cape Coast dance band, The Sugar Babies, were planning to tour Nigeria and invited The Two Bobs to accompany them. Unhappily for the organizer, when all arrangements had been completed for the tour, Ansah and Hutton declined to go, fearing that The Two Bobs might not receive a fair share of the tour earnings. However Bob Johnson chose to go along and the director of the Sugar Babies solved the problem by inviting Charlie Turpin and E.K. Dadson of The Axim Trio to fill the gap. Johnson became The Axim Trio's joker, with Turpin playing the gentleman and Hutton playing Susanna, the lady.

The Nigerian tour was a success and afterwards The Axim Trio stayed together, improving its skills and earning a high reputation for its acting in many towns and villages. In fact the festival celebrations so typical of Ghana seemed always to include a performance by The Axim Trio as a major attraction. For two decades, from 1937 to 1954, the group made itself popular not only in the Gold Coast, but also elsewhere in West Africa, visiting Nigeria (again), Sierra Leone and the Ivory Coast.

Once again, however, the group was not disbanded. Replacements were found that allowed the by now almost legendary Axim Trio to continue its successful touring shows. Dadson's place was at first taken by Mr. Baidoo and shortly after by I.K. Ntiama. Other members also found it difficult to maintain their business commitments against the demands of virtually full-time careers as professional actors, despite the adequate reward from fees collected from the growing audiences. Charlie Turpin was the proprietor of the Hotel de All Stars in Sekondi and had to devote much time to duties there. In 1953 he, too, withdrew from The Axim Trio.

This time the group did not long survive his departure and was disbanded in 1955. The individual members all became involved in private businesses. The decision to disband owed something to the difficulty of replacing by then very popular and well-known comedians. Perhaps, too, there was the feeling that a new approach was required. The concept of the concert party had grown more familiar as it became better known, audiences were demanding an ever greater measure of originality, variety and comic talent from the groups.

Bob Johnson, however, did not give up the stage with the disbanding of The Axim Trio. Theatre was in his blood, for at this point in his life he had already been a comic actor for almost forty years. Without attachment to any particular group, he continued to give individual performances. Occasionally he gave comic shows in front of his small provisions shop to attract customers. But that activity only satisfied him temporarily and he seized the first opportunity to get back to professional acting. The chance came when he was invited to Accra by his former colleagues, Dadson and Turpin, to join a new group which they had formed, called the Worker's Brigade Concert Party. Johnson arrived in Accra on 2 April 1959, and resumed the comic acting which he always referred to as "show business." In 1971 he was still a member and instructor of the Workers' Brigade Drama Group and a leader of one of its sub-groups.

Although comic play-acting was not as lucrative in the 1930s and 1940s as it was to become in the 1960s and early 1970s, The Axim Trio made fairly good money from their performances – an average of 300–400 cedis (¢) from a good night's show. Bob Johnson claims that it was from these earnings that members of The Axim Trio established their private businesses – Dadson's printing press, Turpin's hotel and his own provisions store.

The Axim Trio can rightly be said to have given birth to a host of concert parties which followed it immediately and in that sense to all others in Ghana today. This is evidenced by the popular stage name "Bob" and the group name "Trio" which subsequent comedians and concert parties adopted. To cite a few examples: Bob Cole, Bob Thompson, Bob Vans and such concert parties as The Fanti Trio, The Akan Trio, The Ghana Trio, The Ahanta Trio and so on.

Many of the groups were first formed in the 1940s and early 1950s when there was a rapid proliferation of concert parties which began to tour deeper and deeper into the rural areas in the wake of the popularity of The Axim Trio. One group led by Bob Vans even played to West African troops serving in the Burma campaign during the Second World War.[14] By the early 1950s concert parties were performing exclusively in vernacular languages, particularly the Akan dialects, and instead of more *ad hoc* musical accompaniments, band playing a guitar-band, non-elite style of highlife became an integral part of all concert parties, after the example of E.K. Nyame's Akan Trio formed in 1952.

An overall impression of the quality and variety of the modern concert parties can be gained from an account of the main actors and the particular entertainment which each group provides.

*   *   *

Bob Cole's Group

Bob Cole, whose real name is Kwasi Awotwe, is a leading Ghanaian comedian. He believes he is a born comedian and he gleefully says so when he is asked how and when he learned acting. He and his two schoolmates formed a concert party – The Happy Trio – at Aboso. It functioned for a decade between 1937 and 1947. During school vacations, The Happy Trio used to visit Obuasi, Dunkwa, Bekwai and Kumasi to stage comic plays. As a budding comedian, Bob Cole used to attend the performances of The Axim Trio whenever they performed at Aboso. He admits that he learned some of his techniques from them and at that time he entertained the hope that he and his group would one day succeed The Axim Trio. This hope was later fulfilled.

He completed his elementary education in 1947 and began at once his career of comic acting. He first formed a concert party, named The Jovial Jokers, which became defunct in 1952. For the next two years, until he decided to form a new concert party, The Axim Trio often invited him to accompany them on their tours. In this way he practiced with the original trio, an experience which undoubtedly influenced his technique and the style of his later groups. In 1954 he, Bob Vans and others formed the Ghana Trio, but barely a year later there was some misunderstanding and Bob Vans left to form his own concert party which he also named The Ghana Trio. This resulted in two concert parties of similar name. Bob Cole moved from Sekondi to Accra in April 1956 and adopted a new name for his group. Calling it Bob Cole's Dynamic Ghana Trio, it was this concert party that established Bob Cole's considerable reputation.

According to Bob Cole, before the group had disbanded, all the members were full-time comedians – or, if you will – professional actors. The Trio was a cooperative undertaking from which each member received a share of the profits. Remuneration depended on the money made from audiences during a tour. In spite of difficulties the group made enough money to keep it going for many years.

Although Bob Cole's group no longer exists, Bob Cole has not given up acting. Like Bob Johnson, theatre is in his blood and so he is now a solo actor who performs regularly at the Ambassador Hotel in Accra.

The Fanti Trio

Another offspring of The Axim Trio is The Fanti Trio. It was formed in 1952 by Bob Erick Thompson, John de Heer and Samuel Fletcher at just about the time when the activities of The Axim Trio were nearing an end. These actors, like their predecessors, endeared themselves to comic play-lovers throughout Ghana.

In 1954 The Fanti Trio performed in Accra and were written up in a short but interesting and well-illustrated article in the October issue of *Drum* magazine (West African edition). The editor wrote:

> Oh, what a whooping and yelling there was!...and just because the Fanti Trio were in town. Yes, Erick Thompson, John de Heer and Samuel Fletcher were once again at their "fantics" and in a "fantic" mixture of Fanti and English...[and] wearing fantasy pants they tried to satisfy the Fanti tanticies of their audience.
>
> Then they changed from their Fanti panties to act out the story of the Kayakaya wedding [a *kayakaya* is a

market porter, often "alien," and looked down on by many Ghanaians]. It was a story of love and passion; a story centred round the voluptuous roundness of the beautiful bespectacled Rosina played by our dear Mr. Fletcher. . . . The gist of the story is:

The Kayakaya proposes to a haughty lady called Rosina. She's not flattered, and lets flow a talk of a very straightforward and informal talk about "lice-infested dig" and the like. The talk worries even the Kayakaya, so he goes home and changes into the smartest of smart suits hanging somewhere in his cupboard. And he goes back to win the fair Rosina with a wooing and sighing that the haughty Rosina cannot resist, and they wed.

This extract tells as much about concert parties in general as it does about The Fanti Trio. The simple, almost naive plot of the story is typical of the stories of comic plays which are meant for the man in the street as much as for members of the Ghanaian elite who care to attend them.

Concert parties tend to fall into one of two groups. There are those which began as concert parties and concentrate particularly on acting plays. In these trios, music is only a sideline. Members who are guitarists or instrumentalists and musicians in their own right provide background music and interludes for the comedians and entertain the audience by performing between the plays. Examples of these are the early ones whose history has been outlined above.

In the second category are those that began as groups of musicians. Most common are the guitar bands which were formed with the original aim of providing music and making records for sale. Although enjoying some success as purely musical entertainers, the leaders of these groups later decided to include concert parties in their bands in order to earn more money. The plays were the ingredient that attracted the largest audiences. Concert parties in this category were formed as money-earning subsidiaries to the original guitar bands. The later concert parties which were formed in the 1950s and 1960s such as Kakaiku's concert party, E.K. Nyame's Akan Trio, Kwabena Onyina's Royal Trio, The Happy Stars Band and a host of others fall in this second category.

Musically talented members of concert parties in the first

category provide music for the actors as the mood of the play demands. Members of those in the second group who are competent musicians and either natural or self-taught actors give themselves the extra responsibility of acting in the plays they stage. Kakaiku, in his own band, E.K. Nyame and Okai in E.K.'s Band, and Nortey and Frimpong in The Happy Star Band, provide outstanding examples of such actors. On the other hand, if the original guitar band has no actors some actors may be invited to form a group of actors within the band to perform plays, as has happened with Oyina's Royal Trio. Clearly, no matter how competent and rhythmic the band performances may be, audiences also expect the unique pleasure of the concert party plays during the evening's entertainment.

Kakaiku's Concert Party

Kakaiku's concert party provides a characteristic example of a guitar band which was originally formed to give music at concerts and cut records for money, but later, to increase earnings, added comic plays to the evening's performances. Kakaiku is the pseudonym of its leader, M.K. Oppong, who achieved fame as a guitarist and composer long before he embarked on comic play performances. His songs are particularly enjoyed because of the proverbs they include, and their themes are much enriched with traditional Ghanaian philosophy. In fact, many of his songs are traditional stories skillfully adapted to contemporary Ghanaian highlife tunes which are popular among players and listeners.

M.K. Oppong was born on 2 October 1916 at Aboso, a mining town in the Western Region of Ghana. He attended school, but owing to family problems was unable to complete his education and left in 1932. He worked as a miner from 1939 to 1954. In spite of the harsh life, it was during this period that he learned to play the guitar and began to acquire fame. His skill brought him a considerable reputation as a musician.

He formed his own guitar band in 1954 and his group recorded several songs which were well received by music lovers. His songs were popular, but nevertheless, like other guitarists in his category, the extra financial gains he anticipated spurred him on to transform his band into a concert party. He increased the membership of his band – which at its inception in 1954 consisted of only two guitarists, himself and another musician – by adding a drum player, a maracas player and another player. He also acquired bongos, a jazz drum and electric guitars. The group staged its first play at Aboso and later, using Aboso as its base, toured the country, performing plays.

The admission fee charged by the group in the beginning varied from 10 pesewas to 30 (100 pesewas = ¢1). The average has been increasing over the years, and in the late 1960s it ranged from 60 pesewas (about 25p sterling or 65 American cents) to one cedi (41p or $1.15). This included an entertainment tax of ten percent levied by the government. But expenses kept mounting. According to Kakaiku, in those days when the group hired a house compound, a cinema or a town hall, where it staged its plays, the rent ranged from ¢60 to ¢100. Other concert parties had to meet equally inflated costs.

The present economic crisis in Ghana characterized by galloping inflation makes the 1960 costs miniscule. Presently, concert parties charge admission fees ranging from 20 to 30 pesewas upward per person, yielding daily proceeds ranging from ¢10,000–20,000 a night. But expenses have also mounted. A group now pays on the average about ¢3,000 a day on transportation, about ¢1,000 for renting a small compound or town hall, and where no electricity is available, a small generating plant must be rented at the cost of about ¢600 a night. In addition to these set costs, incidental fees for newspaper and other advertising runs about ¢1,000 a day.

Kakaiku's Concert Party is widely regarded as the best. Its performances always attract a large audience and this demand encouraged its leader to form a second concert party in January 1967. While the first group, with 22 members, performed at various places around Accra, the second party was touring the Western Region. The possibility of using a man's name twice is very attractive financially and, like American road companies, others have copied the arrangement. The late E.K. Nyame was another leader of a concert party that formed a second "road company."

Whereas some of the concert parties that formed in the 1950s and 1960s have now disappeared, Kakaiku's Concert Party is still performing, although due to the current economic state of the country and other factors, its activities have diminished. It is a member of the Musicians Union of Ghana (MUSIA).

The Akan Trio

E.K. Nyame's Akan Trio is a further example of a concert party which began as a guitar band and broadened its entertainment to encompass the money-making comic plays. The Akan Trio was formed about five years after its parent band, the E.K.'s, had been in existence. E.K.'s Band was formed in 1947 but the Trio came much later, in 1952, when Nyame recognized the potential of the comic play.

The late E.K. Nyame, the leader of this band, formed The Akan Trio to cope with an increasing demand for his band's music, yet it was the comic play that added most considerably to his revenue. The financial advantage becomes very apparent when the earnings of the band before and after the formation of the Trio are examined. The fee which the band had been charging for providing music at various functions such as weddings, dances and parties to which they were invited, was ¢2.10 an hour. Thus the total earnings of six hours performance was ¢12.60. With the formation of the concert party they received on the average not less than ¢80 from a six-hour performance. Even when all the extra expenses normally incurred during a performance are deducted, an average of no less than ¢40 profit from a performance remains. This leaves no doubt about the financial gains that followed the development of The Akan Trio from the original band.

The financial earnings of The Akan Trio in great measure accounted for its survival, but the freedom enjoyed by its members made it stable and enabled it to weather the misunderstandings and disagreements that over the years hit many a concert party and led to the splitting up of several of them. According to the leader, the Trio enjoyed a good measure of autonomy within his band. It had its own elected officers, to whom the members were responsible.

The Akan Trio no longer exists. Some of its former members are now playing with newer groups and are thus still active on the concert party scene.

The Royal Trio

The formation of the Royal Trio within Kwabena Onyina's Guitar Band followed a pattern similar to that of the Akan Trio. Onyina, the leader, first formed his band at Agona in Ashanti in 1951. He later moved to Kumasi, where the band flourished and made its mark among Ghanaian guitar music lovers and soon became one of the most popular bands in Ghana. Like the Akan Trio, the Royal Trio that incorporated comic plays, was formed much later, in 1957. Here again, a financial motive prompted its formation. Before it was formed, Onyina's Guitar Band was making ¢12 – ¢16 a performance on such occasions as parties or funeral celebrations and about ¢20 per recording. The value of the recordings was considerably diminished because there was no Ghanaian factory that could handle the processing. The finished records often took up to seven months to arrive from the United Kingdom and become available on the Ghanaian market.

After The Royal Trio was formed, it provided a constant and reliable source of income for the band in addition to the sources enumerated above. The concert party aspect has, in fact, come to dominate the musical entertainment with which the group began. The plays at present are the major source of income for the band, whether they are performed in Accra itself, or on tours of more remote parts of the country.

The Royal Trio now no longer exists, although its leader, Kwabena Onyina, is believed to be making fresh efforts to form a new group.

The Abuakwa Trio

Some of the founders of the concert parties initially joined other guitar bands to prepare themselves for the formation of their own bands. In this way they gained the required experience without having to start from scratch. I.K. Yeboah, the founder of The Abuakwa Trio began like this. He lived at Apedwa near Kibi, in the Eastern Region, where he worked as a tailor. He joined Apea Agyekum's band in 1940, but did not form a trio of his own until years later. The earnings of his trio were initially very encouraging, according to Yeboah, but it became defunct because the parents and relatives of some of its members disapproved of their association with the group.

The reason for this attitude must be explained. There was of course the usual concern about the irresponsible nature of the itinerant life of a traveling musician, but there was also objection to the actual instrument, the guitar. It was considered particularly reprehensible, and evidence of degeneration in the one who played it. This is because in Ghana, the playing of a guitar used to be generally associated with drunkeness and other social vices. Parents and relatives advised their sons and wards against it. Today such unfavorable notions about guitar playing are fast dying out.

Rather than battle against their families' expressed disapproval, members lost interest in The Abuakwa Trio's activies and drifted off into other activities. This disintegration did not occur all at once, and the group maintained a popular reputation for some time. But eventually and inevitably it did collapse and with the demise of his own trio, Yeboah rejoined Apea Agyekum's Band in 1961. He left in 1965 to join the Brigade Drama Group, of which he is still a member, but he no longer manages a trio in his own name.

However, since 1965 a lot has happened in the interesting history of concert parties, including the Brigade Drama Group which still exists but does not bear its original name because it is now a constituent member of a national company. It is one of three groups – the Brigade Drama Group, the Puppetry Theatre, and the Drumming and Dancing Group – that make up the National Folkloric Company of the Ghana Arts Centre.

During an interview in early 1984 with Mr. Yeboah at the Arts Centre, he indicated not only how much he enjoyed his 19 years with the Brigade Drama Group but also reminisced about the activities of concert parties generally over the years. He commented, "Since our group joined the National Folkloric Company, I have enjoyed my dramatic activities all the more because I have appeared in many television and public shows, and that has made me more popular. But these days, 'the money is not coming' as it used to."

The Happy Stars Band

Messrs. Nortey and Frimpong, two leading members of The Happy Stars Band, also began their professional careers like I.K. Yeboah. They joined other concert parties before forming their own bands. They first joined The All Stars Band and when it became defunct, Nortey joined The Fanti Trio and Frimpong became a member of the Jaguar Jokers.

Nortey's desire to start his own guitar band grew daily, and in 1957 he and some friends, including Frimpong, formed a band called The Happy Stars in memory of the band he and Frimpong had first joined. At this time, the band not only provided music for concert parties, but also recorded songs for the Philips Record Company. After an argument over the ownership of musical instruments and other equipment, which resulted in the original patron seizing the equipment, the band dissolved and its members joined Bob Cole's group, The Ghana Trio. They named their band The Ghana String Band and, although successful, they still felt an allegiance to their first venture. So, while they were members of The Ghana Trio, they recorded songs under the name of The Happy Stars Band. Their songs became so popular among Ghanaians that Nortey and Frimpong made a second attempt to reorganize The Happy Stars Band, this time in 1958.

They were joined by T.D.B Agyekum, through whom they were able to obtain financial backing from a Mr. Kyei, a businessman from Kumasi, who paid for their musical instruments and equipment. In appreciation of his gesture, he was made patron and Mr. Agyekum was made leader of the band – although Nortey and Frimpong were clearly the musical innovators of the group. The band's records sold well, and the group (and Mr. Kyei) profited. Yet in spite of this apparent success, both in reputation and financially, it was still reckoned that greater profit could be made by adding comic actors to the act. This was done, and in the following years, The Happy Stars Band enjoyed enthusiastic response from audiences throughout the country.

Despite success and popularity, the band carried onerous financial liabilities due to the loan made by Mr. Kyei for the company equipment. Payment to Mr. Kyei was made on account each week, and in due course ownership of the equipment would have become theirs outright. However, financial bad luck continued to plague The Happy Stars Band. In 1966 the group hired a truck from a Syrian in Agona Swedru with the object of playing to new and what they anticipated would be large audiences. Unfortunately, the tour coincided with the beginning of the rainy season and unexpectedly meager audiences turned out. It must be realized that performances in the smaller towns were usually given in the open air. As a result of poor gate receipts, the band was unable to cover the cost of renting the truck, and the Syrian had a lien placed on the musical instruments, equipment and costumes, thereby depriving the band of its livelihood. It became so disorganized that Agyekum reluctantly departed, but Nortey and Frimpong remained undaunted. They managed to scrape together sufficient funds to pay off the Syrian and redeem their equipment, and once again The Happy Stars Band were performing. Now, Nortey was the leader, and the newly reorganized company employed additional musicians, making it, at 15 members, a large group. General arrangements and plan remained the same. Like other concert parties, members took a proportional share of the receipts at the end of each tour. Each member's share depended on the total income and on his position in the band. For instance, if the leader received ₵3,000, the next ranking member received 2,500, and the next ₵2,000, and so on.

Unlike some of the old time concert parties that have disbanded, The Happy Stars Band still exists, although it does not appear as active as it used to be.

An Attempt at National Organization

The individual history of these selected concert parties has been given because it indicates the general pattern of development of the numerous concert parties in Ghana today. In 1974 there were well over thirty guitar bands which also operated as concert parties. Now, a decade later, there are about an equal number (see the list below) performing throughout Ghana and outside the country. Like every human activity in Ghana, the activities of concert parties have been affected by the recent economic situation. The groups' travels are sometimes delayed because of lack of gasoline, and when gasoline is available at the beginning of a tour, there may be difficulty in obtaining fuel at later stops. Mounting costs have increased the average admission charge to 30 cedis a person, and by careful planning of itineraries and local advertising in newspapers and by posters, concert parties have managed to turn a profit. Some travel to neighboring Ivory Coast, Liberia, and Nigeria for engagements, and groups such as F. Kenya's Band and Nananom's Band are said to travel abroad a couple of times a year.

The popular appeal of comic plays has led to the formation of a series of new companies. The increasing financial return that could be earned urged Mr. Kobina Sagoe to form the Ghana National Entertainment Association in 1960. Sagoe saw the financial potential of this field, but he also appreciated, perhaps better than the groups themselves, the kind of difficulties of organization into which the rapidly multiplying groups might run. His Association might be seen as an agency and even a registry or a kind of trade union of the concert parties. It offered the groups the security and strength that comes with association and allowed each group to share the experiences of others and to learn of potential areas of profit and difficulty that might be encountered. In its opening year, 1960, there were 28 guitar bands registered as members of the association. These were:

Agyeren's Band
Ahamano's Band
Ahanta Trio
Akan Trio's Band No. 2
Amaning's Band
Appiah Adjekum's Band
Armah's Band
Asare's Band
Baya Jokers
Bioson's Band
Black Star Trio
Bob Cole's Ghana Trio
Builder's Brigade Concert
Party
Danleo's Concert Party
E.K.'s Akan Trio No. 1
Fanti Trio (Sampson's Band)
I.E. Maison's Band
Jaguar Jokers
Kakaiku's Band
Kwaa Mensah's Band
Kwabena Kyem's Band
Kwasi Effusah's Band
Kwasi Twe's Band
Morocco Jokers Band
Onyina's Guitar Band
(Royal Trio)
Sam's Band
T.D. Quarcoo's Band
Yaw Kuma's Band

As the constitution clearly indicated, the Association aimed at encouraging Ghanaian musicians and actors to improve their arts.

It also indicated its intention to serve as a central body which would supervise the activities of the member bands. A series of competitive performances was one of the practical steps taken by the Association to improve the performances of its members. From two to six members competed at a time. They were each required to stage a play within a limited time before a panel who ranked the bands in order of merit. The band which won the first place was given a handsome silver cup and other winners received appropriate trophies. The first of these series of competitions was held at Agona Swedru Sports Stadium on 4 March 1961. The competing bands were six in number: the Ahanta Trio, the Fanti Trio, I.E. Maison's Band, Bob Cole's Ghana Trio, Kakaiku's Band, and E.K.'s Akan Trio No. 1.

In spite of obvious and manifold advantages, the Association might have seemed to be able to offer its members, considerable difficulty was experienced in bringing people together and forming an effective general policy appropriate for all. Perhaps the difficulty of uniting the growing, heterogenous collection of aspiring and competitive individual artists was an impossible task from the beginning. And one may, therefore, ask whether it was necessary or merely a reflection on centralizing tendencies in the Ghanaian body politic of the time. Without any decisive activity, however, the Association inevitably became defunct towards the end of 1966. In spite of the high ideals of its constitution, it was not performing any useful functions for its members, most of whom increasingly preferred to continue along their individualistic ways.

For well over a decade from 1966 until 1978 no further attempt was made to form a mutual association of concert parties on similar lines. If there is some overall advantage in being able to call upon a single (and effective) spokesman, the indifference of the leaders towards such a body is evidence of their extreme individuality that represents the originality and personal skills of the artist, the 1966 disintegration of the Association was probably artistically advantageous. Yet it seems that further support of the Association might have given it that true authority on which could rest the power to seek significant economic advantages for the mixed collection of bands and concert parties which it sought to represent for several years.

Unity is strength, and the individual artists of the various concert parties have always been aware of that fact. It came as no surprise therefore when on Saturday, 24 June 1978, the knell was tolled of their rugged individualism. That day witnessed the promulgation of the constitution that established the Musicians Union Of Ghana [MUSIGA] of which all concert parties are registered members. The membership of MUSIGA, which covers most all musical groups and artists, includes the following concert parties among registered members. They are:

Abeshie Concert Troup
Adom Professionals Band (a newly formed all-blind group)
African Brothers Internationals Band
Agyaba's Band
Akonoba's Band
Alex Konadu's Band
All Brothers Band
Ashanti Brothers International Band
City Boys Internationals Band
Cubano Fiestas Band
F. Kenya's Band
F. Micah's Band
Happy Stars Band
Jaguar Jokers Band
K.K.'s No. 2 Band
Kakaiku's Band
Kumapim Royals Band
Kusum Agoromba
Nananom Band
Nteaseie Band
Oketekyie's Band
Okukuseku's Internationals Band
Okyeame Bediako and the Sensationals Band
Osofo Dadzie Group
Senior Eddie Donkor and the Internationals Band
Sunsum Mystic Band
Yaanom Professionals Band
Yamoah's Band

The central objective of the defunct Ghana National Entertainment Association and the Musicians of Ghana, namely, the safeguarding of members interests as well as helping them to improve their arts is clearly spelled out in their constitutions. As compared

F. Micah's concert party on the road in Ghana.

The stock comic characters comic appearance is enhanced by minstrel make-up.

with the earlier constitution, the preamble to MUSIGA'S constitution is somewhat more pan-Africanist. It reads:

> We, the Musicians of Ghana and of Africa, having realized the great potential in music and having accepted that this potential is not being employed in the interest of musicians, and having found that musicians are being exploited everywhere, and having found that musicians do not obtain full benefits for their endeavors, and having found that musicians in spite of their worthy contributions are not accorded their rightful place in society,
>
> Now hereby resolve to establish by this constitution an organization strong and flexible to promote the best interests of music and musicians of Ghana and Africa.

This principal objective is spelt out in detail in the following thirteen aims and objectives:

- To protect the creative and performing rights of all musicians in the country.
- To arrest and contain the exploitation of musicians of Ghana and elsewhere.
- To ensure a fair return for the efforts of all musicians in Ghana.
- To encourage a healthy growth of the music industry in Ghana.
- To encourage musical talent.
- To seek and maintain the best interests of musicians.
- To promote research into indigenous music and culture.
- To affiliate with all organizations which seek to promote the well-being of musicians.
- To cater for retired musicians and or provide unemployment benefits for members.
- To seek to bring practising musicians into this Union.
- To accord musicians an honourable place in the society.
- To build a union hall, headquarters, theatre halls, etc.

To raise and maintain high standards of conduct for
    practising musicians in Ghana.

Through its laudable aims and objectives, MUSIGA hoped to in-
spire its membership to unflagging support and to a degree that the
earlier Association lacked. In this way it may well become an effective spokesman for and protector of Ghana's artists and musicians.

2
The Actors, The Comedians

As mentioned earlier, comedians in concert parties were all men until recently. The stage is considered an unsuitable career for moral young women. As in Shakespeare's England, it falls to younger men to play women's parts, and likewise also this is one of the extra amusements for the audience. In Shakespeare's *As You Like It*, for example, Rosalind pretends to be Ganymede on the stage. Since Rosalind was played by a boy actor, the boy thus pretended to be a girl pretending to be a boy. Quite a lot of the wit is written around this ludicrous situation in which the actors are, as characters, deceived at one level believing the girl is a boy while the audience is aware at another level that the girl is a boy in the first place. This practice of dressing up as a woman in concert parties enhances the comic nature of the plays. The audience is amused to see a man dressed in female clothes and behaving in every way like a Ghanaian woman. Some of them are such effective female mimics that at night, when dressed up in feminine garments, they could easily be mistaken for women.

As is to be expected, the parts or roles the actors play are largely determined by their appearance. Young men with fresh cheeks, whose "handsomeness" resembles the beauty of Ghanaian women, are selected to play the parts of young ladies or women in the plays. Fairly elderly comedians whose wisdom and experience enable them to play the parts of old men and women, often the parents of the young women, are assigned those parts. A very good example of an elderly comedian who plays the part of old women with extraordinary exactness is the veteran and renowned Ghanaian composer, Kakaiku (M.K. Oppong), who is a leader of his own guitar band. Another example of a player who acts the part of an old woman very well is Bob Cole, whose real name is Kwasi Awotwe. Bob Cole's distinction as an actor is so well recognized that in 1964 he was chosen as the gold medalist by the Ghanaian *Sunday Mirror* newspaper for his excellent performances as a comedian.

However, nowadays actresses are recruited to perform the parts of women whenever a band can afford to expand its membership. This change has come about as a result of increased participation of women in new cultural activities and partly in response to the national theatre movement which has given rise to a number of new drama groups with male and female members but which are not in the concert party tradition. Some of these new groups, such as the Brigade Drama Group and the Kusum Agoromma, use the concert party dramatic form as well as other styles of dramatic presentation.

In general, concert party comedians do not receive any formal training in acting, though some learning is acquired through a kind of apprenticeship system. A person is either a born comedian or else he learns to become one simply by watching other comedians trying out their skills in the parts.

Opportunities for learning the art of the concert party comedian arise during rehearsals, for it is customary for many concert parties to rehearse the plays in the presence of other members of the band who in turn act as a critical audience. They watch and correct any unsatisfactory parts of the play and satisfy themselves that the performance of the new comedian is good enough before presentation to the general public. This is the only element of training that the comedians have. Their suggestions and comments are impromptu but highly effective and so are their professional methods of guidance. For the actor's peers are not theorists but understand from personal experience what works on the stage. Thus, their expectations are highly pragmatic and realistic.

Despite the handicap of the lack of prior study and training in the art of acting, a close observation of a comedian during his performances reveals the characteristics and qualities which make a successful comedian: for example, histrionic abilities and temperament. He should be able to simulate the behavior and actions of the characters he represents in a convincing manner, highlighting any aspects that can arouse immediate audience reaction. He should have a good singing voice and a knack for selecting suitable songs to punctuate his statements. Above all, he should be proficient in dancing and must be able to dance the latest styles of the highlife and introduce suitable embellishments. Each come-dian possesses these qualities to a varying degree.

It is clear that the talents of these actors are manifold. All of them have the original essential ability to crack jokes. Some of them joke incessantly, and they indulge in buffoonery and slap-stick activities that can throw an audience into fits of laughter. To heighten the humor, comedians are careful to remain deadpan and never to laugh themselves, no matter how extreme audience laughter may become. Their lugubrious and contrasting solem-nity makes the clowning seem all the funnier to an audience al-ready delighted by the joke. Most of the comic actors have good singing voices. They have suitable songs ready and sing them dur-ing their performance at just the opposite moment. In this way, the songs appear to have been deliberately written for the play. It is by means of song that the sentiments and feelings of the audi-ence are aroused. On many occasions individuals are so carried away by the emotions induced by sentimental songs that, without waiting for a suitable interval, they rush up to the stage and offer gifts (three, five or ten pesewas) even while he is still performing.

Players, like actors from any other parts of the world, are re-quired to memorize their parts, but as comic plays are never actu-ally written down, they must also be adept at improvization. Quick-wittedness is especially valuable, for an actor can generate additional enthusiasm and humor by inserting comic and familiar local references within the events of the standard play per-formance.

The repertoire may vary, and some actors manage to play a vari-ety of parts effectively, from old men to rustic farmers. A young actor must be capable of realistically portraying an innocent maiden or a "good time" girl.

Because situations depicted in comic plays are familiar and con-temporary, the costumes worn by the actors are not unusual. Realism rather than spectacle is the aim. Occasionally, they can be dramatic in their exaggeration of the ordinary. Usually, how-ever, actors simply dress themselves in a manner that will im-mediately suggest to the audience the role they seek to portray. For this effect, comedians' costumes range from the very shabby to the most fashionable clothes in current use. The players dress exactly as the characters they represent might do, and costumes become part of the attempt at verisimilitude. But since the plays

Actors are primarily responsible for making the audience enjoy itself, but the plays also exhibit dramatic moments, such as the scene portrayed here, in which a "hunter" threatens to decapitate a "city slicker."

themselves are only one part of the whole evening's entertainment, when they open the show with music and song, they wear quite different costumes which are often colorful and even ridiculous. These might be long-sleeved shirts with white stripes or lace. Sometimes caps with words like "Bob," "Sharp," and "OK" embroidered on them are worn. Similar words may be written on an actor's shirt front. Each actor may wear canvas shoes of different unmatched colors. A comedian may wear one white canvas shoe and one black or brown one to appear more eccentric and absurd.

When the play itself begins, a variety of clothes is worn. Comedians who play the parts of a farmer and his family from the rural areas of Ghana dress as the real characters would. The farmer may appear in threadbare clothes, with a cutlass tucked under his armpit and an old bag in his hand. His wife also may wear old clothes, while her headdress may be worn in a style typical of village women. Their daughter may be shabbily dressed, and, depicting a youthful desire to appear attractive, she may resort to a laughable imitation of city girls by smearing her face with excessive powder. Their appearance and rustic behavior leave the audience in no doubt as to who they are.

The dresses of actors who perform the parts of "good time" girls or ladies from the towns and cities attract attention because, as is appropriate, they are far more elaborate. On the stage actors wear all the finery typical of the profession they are copying. They wear changes of clothes and fashionable and stylish dresses. Even their hairdoes are exact copies of those worn by "good time" girls.

A comedian playing the role of a gentleman or a white-collar worker may wear a fashionable suit tailored in the latest style. When church priests appear in a play, the actors wear a fair imitation of the clothes of real priests. If one is playing a priest of the Methodist or Presbyterian Church, he dresses in the usual black suit with a white collar around his neck and carries a Holy Bible in his hand. If he is a priest of a sect of the Apostolic Churches, he wears a long white robe with a broad red cotton strip around his waist and carries a wooden cross in his hand. Similarly, if he is a traditional priest, he wears among other things a specially woven raffia skirt and arm and foot bands, carrying small bells that tinkle when he dances. He wears talismen around his neck and feet, and his attendants throw ground white clay at his feet and his face.

If actors are performing in a play with a funeral celebration, they wear the most current Ghanaian mourning clothes. On the other hand, when a chief is celebrating his annual festival, such as the one in the story of Cinderella adapted to the African background, with the title "Treat Somebody's Child as Your Own," the actor wears a rich *kente* cloth, a headband, a regal pair of sandals and golden rings and sits in state with his elders and retinue of followers around him. In short, he demonstrates the mood and displays all the pomp and pageantry characteristic of the occasion.

3
Humor In The Plays

Concert parties exploit all avenues for appealing to the humor of their audiences and their sense of the comic. They use humorous language, make unexpected statements, crack jokes and tell humorous anecdotes while ensuring that the main story and theme of the play are reaching the audience. They also exploit movement and dance for similar effects and, above all, put much thought into costume and make-up.

As a rule the costumes that are selected are considered not only in relation to characterization but also in relation to the overriding interest of concert parties in the comic. Players go in for both realism and fantasy. When they want to be realistic, they make every effort to dress exactly as the characters they represent would. Indeed sometimes they are deliberately over-realistic.

A play's humor is created in numerous ways. Unexpected and sometimes meaningless references to everyday things, places and incidents, often at the wrong time and place, amuse an audience. A comedian may refer to a fellow comedian dressed like an old woman as "Abrewa No Parking," that is, "Old Lady No Parking," referring to a common road sign found in towns in Ghana. An actor may then use the same phrase "No Parking" to describe a situation in which he finds himself in the play. Finding himself in a wretched condition with almost no clothes to wear, he may say, "It is owing to my kindness and generosity that I have now found myself in this No Parking." A comedian may refer to God as "Old Man," a common Ghanaian term for one's father or, as it really means, an elderly man. He may also speak of a man who has died as having "gone on a transfer," a term that is usually employed in Ghana to signify when an employer decrees a move in his employee's place of work. Another term often used by comedians is "counter-back," meaning a police station, and in this case, a metaphor. The counter in the police station is the one behind which people under arrest are often detained for questioning, and it is made to stand for the police station itself. A comedian may tell his audience how, as a villager, he one day visited Accra, Kumasi, and Takoradi, and, ignorant of city life, got into trouble by following city boys and finally found himself at a "counter-back."

The comedians' funny and ridiculous remarks, statements, and dances sustain the humor throughout the play. The audience is amused to hear, for instance, an actor recounting how even if a late relation failed to send a message that he was going to die before doing so, he nevertheless left a daughter behind for him to care for. The precise way in which he presents the joke is Ghanaian, but his sense of the unexpected and the improbable is appreciated world-wide as humor.

The language, or rather, languages, used in a comic drama contribute a great deal to the overall humor. This is popular drama, and the actors therefore employ the local language to the full, taking advantage of particular characteristic idioms. Fante and Twi, two Akan dialects, are most often used by comedians. This is because Akans have been concerned most often with "composing" comic plays. This dominance is likely to change in the course of time, and other Ghanaian languages may well come into use. Occasional letters to the Ghanaian daily papers from non-Akan comic playgoers already demand that other Ghanaian languages be used in staging plays. To the extent that it is audience demand that ultimately decides what is going to be presented, it is likely that comic actors from other than the Fante- and Twi-speaking areas will soon begin to offer plays. The success of concert parties today in the two major and established languages points the way.

Yet even when audiences require and enjoy plays in their own language, it will surely still be recognized that certain features of Twi and Fante make them ideal for comic plays.

The apparent appropriateness of the two Akan dialects for this purpose may not derive only from the fact that all the plays at present have been developed in these dialects. The typical and effective form of these plays can, after all, only be measured against established varieties, yet linguistic tradition does have certain peculiar features. These Akan dialects are rich in humorous expressions which make them especially suitable for comic plays and make them perfect vehicles for comedians. In addition, the occasional use of pidgin English and what may be termed "faulty"

A "chief," dressed in rich *kente* cloth, is being "congratulated" by his followers.

Twi adds to the humor. The actor who speaks pidgin usually plays the part of a houseboy or a steward – the kind of person whom the African rather than the foreigner generally regards as speaking pidgin English. On the other hand, an actor who speaks "faulty" Twi appears as either a Yoruba or a Mossi. Of all non-Akan, the Yoruba and the Mossi are noted for speaking Twi with marked intonations and thus their Twi is exceedingly amusing to the Twi. A comedian who has learnt to copy that version of Twi does so to amuse his audience.

There is usually among comedians someone who can speak and act in a funnier way than any other comedian in his group. He contributes the greater or at least a more significant part of the total effort which actors make to entertain their audience. His role in a comic play is somewhat similar to that of a typical clown or jester in a Shakespearean play.

Laughter is evoked in particular ways. A rustic farmer visiting his daughter and son-in-law may light a candle which he has taken to their house where there are electric lights. His son-in-law draws attention to his odd behavior. Realizing the oddity of using a candle in a room lit by electric lights, the father-in-law will suddenly extinguish it amidst laughter from the audience who are themselves happily familiar with both forms of illumination.

38

An actor playing the part of a rival woman or a man or his wife may work himself up into a frenzy and resort to angry speeches defying and accusing in such a strain of eloquence that the audience, finding it familiar, can hardly contain its amusement. If women rivals happen to be quarreling, their verbal contest can suddenly turn into a physical one and they fight in a way typical of Ghanaian women in this situation: each hits her palms against those of the other. Rival wives may rock their husband between them. If the rivals are men and one of them is an old man, he adopts an amusing way of fighting, caricaturing a boxer. He will stagger after every blow he gives and sometimes fall prostrate on the stage when his blow misses his opponent.

Or, a stern father might cause considerable laughter when he asks his daughter why she has stayed out late at night. He will pull his hand from his cloth to reveal a table clock tied around his wrist on which he begins to demonstrate the hour of the night when she was where one should not be. In another example, a Ghanaian priest who has returned from Britain where he trained pretends that he can no longer understand nor speak Fante. He therefore conducts all his sermons in English and has them interpreted into Fante by an interpreter. When commenting on the omniscience of God in a sermon, the priest asks a rhetorical question, "Who knows, nobody knows, only God knows." The interpreter presumes that he has heard the priest say, "Whose nose, it's nobody's nose, it's only God's nose," and he interprets it accordingly. The priest is only then compelled to shout in Fante, amidst great laughter from the audience, "That is not what I said, I said . . ." This is the humor that follows when the conceit of self-deception is exposed to ridicule. It is a theme that has long been popular among actors seeking to amuse Fante audiences.

Members of the audience cannot but laugh when a comedian remarks of another comedian, "He is handsome, but it is just because today is Thursday that he looks ugly. You wait and see how handsome he will look on Friday." As if that were not enough to make the audience laugh, he may turn to another comedian and say, "You are not handsome at all, if ever you come across a dead person who is handsome, do exchange your ugliness for his handsomeness."

Humanity needs to laugh – the Ghanaian not least. It has been well said that all the world loves a clown.

4
Music And Dancing

Not only humor but also music and dancing form an essential and conspicuous feature of comic plays, contributing much of their value, meaning, and attraction. Some playgoers attend plays principally to enjoy the ear-catching music so plentifully provided by the comic bands. Indeed, music is as vital a part of the plays as it is of American musicals.

Music

The bands use African and Western musical instruments. The equipment of a typical concert party includes an electric guitar, an amplifier, a loudspeaker, a microphone, clappers, maracas, tom-toms, and donno bongos and a jazz drum set comprising: side drum, bass drum, alto drum, cymbals and trap. When these instruments are skillfully played to blend well with the singing of Ghanaian highlife and other songs, they produce a most effective music enlivening the plays and making them more enjoyable. The songs frequently used in the plays fall into two broad categories: sentimental and philosophical.

Sentimental songs are mainly about love and loved ones: songs about the importance of love and how love surpasses riches – love songs which lovers sing in admiration of their loved ones, to express their longing for their sweethearts and to indicate how inseparable they are. Their themes are the universal romanticism common to all pop music. A typical example of the sentimental type of song in comic plays follows below. It is a Twi song which a person longing for his lover would sing. As can be seen from the text below, it is phrased in repetitive but highly emotional language conveying a short but important love message from an ardent lover to her sweetheart. The singer does not think life is worth living without her lover and she threatens to die if the lover fails to come to her. Since this song is often sung by "good time" ladies, it also contains a note of expectation and even insincerity.

A guitarist and a group of singers performing during a concert party.

Woamma a Mewu by E.K.'s Akan Band

Woamma a, mewu, woamma a mewu odo!
Woamma, mewu, odo maye mmobo.
Woamma a, mewu, woamma a mewu odo!
Woamma a, mewu, odo maye mmobo.
Awereho kum Sunsum odo, woamma a, mewu.

Woho adwendwen na adooso o!
Woamma a mewu, woamma a mewu.
Daben na mehu wo anim?

> *Chorus*
> Woamma a, mewu, woamma a, mewu,
> Woamma a, mewu, odo maye mmobo.
> Woamma a, mewu, woamma a, mewu.
> Woamma a, mewu, odo maye mmobo.

Awereho kum sunsum, odo, woamma a, mewu.
Ade rekye na ade resa yi, woamma a, mewu.
Wo ho adwendwen na adooso o!
Woamma a mewu, woamma a, mewu.
Daben na mehu wo anim?

> *Chorus*
> Woamma a, mewu, woamma a, mewu, etc.

41

(English Text)
I Shall Die If You Don't Come

I shall die if you don't come,
   I shall die if you don't come, darling.
I shall die if you don't come;
   darling, I am miserable.
I shall die if you don't come,
   I shall die if you don't come.
I shall die if you don't come;
   darling, I am miserable.

Sadness dampens the human spirit;
   I shall die if you don't come, darling.
I have been thinking about you all the time;
I shall die if you don't come,
   I shall die if you don't come.
When shall I expect to see you?

     Chorus
     I shall die if you don't come,
        I shall die if you don't come.
     I shall die if you don't come;
        darling, I am miserable.
     I shall die if you don't come,
        I shall die if you don't come;
     I shall die if you don't come;
        darling, I am miserable.

Sadness dampens the human spirit;
   I shall die if you don't come, darling.
As the days go by, I shall die if you don't come.
I have been thinking about you all the time.
I shall die if you don't come,
   I shall die if you don't come.
When shall I expect to see you?

     Chorus
     I shall die if you don't come,
        I shall die if you don't come, etc.

The philosophical category, as may be imagined, embraces a wide range of songs. It covers songs of the sorrows and sufferings of orphans and how only God cares for them; the ungratefulness of men; the evil machinations of kith and kin and trusted friends; the vicissitudes of life on earth and so forth. The following is an example:

Onuapa Due by K. Akwaboa's Band

Onuapa due O!
Onuapa due, due ne amanehunu.
Wiase mu a yewo yi, wo ni wu a, na w'abusua asa
Ena awu ama asem ato me o!
Asem to me a, gyefo ne hwane?
Abusua ayi me o! obaakofo ee, due o!
Mede m'asem ama Onyame o!

Awisiaba ee, gyae su
Awisiaba ee, gyae su, na wusu a, nnisuo besa.
Wiase a yewo yi, wo ni wu a, na w'abusua asa.
Ena awu ama asem ato me o!
Asem to me a gyefo ne hwane?
Abusua ayi me o! obaakofo ee, due o!
Mede m'asem ama Onyame o!

Wisase mu a yewo yi, agyanka asem ye mmobo se
Ekom de agyanka a, yese a oyare.
Nye yare na oyare, se wiase mu a yewo yi,
Mpanyinfo bu be se obaatan na onim
   dee ne ba bedie
Eno saman pa ee, eye a, behwe me e!

> *Chorus*
> Meme Awoe obi r'ba a, man' me o!
> Obir'ba a, man' me
> Agyankaba ee, obi r'ba a, man' me
> Obir'ba a man' me,
> Adee ahia me o obi r'ba a man' me
> Obir'ba a, man' me.

(English Text)

Good Fellow, condolences!
Good Fellow, condolences;
   condolence, on your suffering!
The death of one's mother deprives one of
   one's family ties in this world;
A mother's death has brought suffering upon me.
Who will rescue me in time of suffering?
My kinsfolk have thrown me out!
A person without kinsfolk, condolences!
I leave my suffering to God.

Weep not, orphan!
Weep not, orphan!
   You will drain tears by weeping.
The death of one's mother deprives one of
   one's family ties in this world.
A mother's death has brought suffering upon me.
Who will rescue me in time of suffering?
My kinsfolk have thrown me out.
Give condolences to a person without kinsfolk.
I leave my suffering to God.

An orphan is miserable in this world;
When hungry he is considered unwell –
It is not that he is unwell.
There is an old proverb which says that
'It is the mother who knows what her child
   desires to eat' in this world.
Good spirit of my mother, come to my rescue!

    Chorus
    Mother, send me gifts when there
      is somebody coming!
    Send me gifts when there is somebody coming!
    I am needy! Send me gifts when there
      is somebody coming!
    Send me gifts when there is somebody coming!

In contrast to the sentimental song, this philosophical ditty continually relates to the Ghanaian kinship system, especially that based on matrilineal inheritance. Under Ghanaian kinship, a member of a family can always count on other members to help him in time of need or difficulty. All members of a family are so obliged by custom and tradition. Rather paradoxically, it is equally true that a person's position in the corporate unit of the Ghanaian family is weakened if and when his mother dies. Thenceforth, due regard may not be given to his rights within the family. In an extreme case, none of his kinsmen will bother to ask about him or look after his welfare. Such a situation is particularly miserable for a person who is not only an orphan but has lost all his relatives.

It is on such misfortune that the song philosophizes, whilst depicting the sufferings and hardships which an orphan and a person who has no kindred endures in the world. Such a song, when sung at a timely point in the course of a comic play, can deeply move an audience.

The recordings of any band, registered on discs for sale, become more meaningful when they are sung in a comic play. Thus the song "Awisiaba ye mmobo" ("An Orphan is Pitiable") cannot fail to make an impression on the audience when sung by Mansa in the play entitled "Treat Somebody's Child as Your Own." The ill-treatment which Mansa suffers from her stepmother and two half-sisters provides a fitting background for the song. As described in the story, Nkatiaba, the stepmother, discriminates between her own two daughters and Mansa. She gives her daughters good clothes to wear, while Mansa wears the same shabby cloth all the time. Mansa does all the domestic chores, including cooking, while the two beloved daughters enjoy themselves. In one scene, when Mansa finishes cooking and sends the food to Nkatiaba, she gives her two daughters some of the food to eat and sends Mansa to sweep the kitchen before eating her share. On her return, Mansa finds that her two half-sisters have eaten most of her share of the food and have poured water into what remained. On discovering this, Mansa weeps bitterly, singing the song, "An Orphan is Pitiable."

Any member of the audience who before seeing the play might seldom have considered the pitiable condition in which an orphan sometimes finds himself or herself gains a vivid and memorable dramatization. The comedians demonstrate their resourcefulness by making it a point to use songs that fit well into the stories of their plays. They search their repertoire and are even impelled to compose new ones or rephrase and change the rhythm of traditional songs to serve their purpose. Comic plays certainly provide a rewarding opportunity for creative work in African music.

The concert parties reflect current Ghanaian social problems and happenings, not only in the play they perform, but also in the songs they compose. In the songs they philosophize on the social situation and give expression to social ideas, feelings and moods; and through the songs, they give currency to pithy expressions and catchwords which become popular among the masses and sometimes also among the elite of Ghanaian society. The ideas are given broad as well as individual interpretations by the people. Two song hits by the African Brothers' Band, recorded in the mid-60s, during a period of political turbulence, may be described here in illustration of this point.

The first of the two song hits which were composed in 1966 post-coup Ghana is entitled "Okwaduo" (wild ox). It is based on an interesting story that runs thus: Once upon a time, a hunter and his two wives lived in a village. To supplement his hunting, the hunter set traps. It was his habit to kill all animals he trapped before taking them home. One day, his wives told him not to kill any animal which he would find alive in his trap. He should bring it home to be reared. Good husband that he was, he accepted the suggestion of his wives and decided to do what they had told him.

A day or two after his wives' suggestion, the hunter trapped a wild ox (*okwaduo*) and made up his mind to take it home alive to be reared. But he wanted to make sure that the animal would not escape when taken out of the trap. "Will you run away when I take you out of the trap or will you follow me home?" asked the hunter. "Oh, no! Why should I?" said the wild ox; "You know better than I do that everybody desires life in this world, because life is sweet. I shan't run away if you free me from your trap, I shall follow you home," the animal added. Thereupon the hunter took the wild ox out of the trap and, to his great surprise and dismay, the wild ox immediately took to its heels, telling the hunter, "You won't catch me; not this year at least." Dumbfounded and almost mesmerized by the behavior of the wild ox, the hunter cursing and swearing said: "Well, you are gone, but woe be to your brothers if they fall into my trap."

The song was composed soon after the 1966 February coup and the general interpretation which was and still is given to the theme is that the ousted President Nkrumah, who was out of Ghana at the time of the coup, was fortunate to have escaped the anger of Ghanaians while his close associates and followers, who were in Ghana during the coup, had to suffer the brunt of the people's anger. They were subjected to protective custody; commissions of enquiries were set up to examine their assets; and some were disqualified from holding public offices. The main statement of the song, "You are gone, but woe be to your brothers," became a popular phrase which was always on the lips of people from all walks of life. The philosophy of the song so fascinated one prominent Ghanaian that he bought the record so that he could hear it as often as he wished.

The second song is also based on an interesting and meaningful story. It is entitled "Ebi te Yie" ("Some Are Well Seated"). Readers may note that the expression *"Ebi te yie"* can also be understood as "Some are living well." The song tells how once upon a time there was a general meeting of all animals, including the leopard and duiker. It happened that the leopard sat right behind the duiker and subjected it to unbearable bullying and ill-treatment while the meeting was in progress. First, the leopard pinned down the tail of the duiker with his claws and he would not allow the latter to participate in the deliberations. As soon as the duiker began to speak, the leopard would shout him down and tell him that the meeting was not for small animals; or he would hit him on the head and tell him that he was talking too much.

The bullying and intimidation became so agonizing that the duiker could not bear it; he shouted, "petition please, on a point of order, chairman, secretary, gentlemen, honorable members of the meeting, we have had some deliberations since the meeting began. I would suggest we adjourn it until another day because not all of us are well or comfortably seated at this meeting. Some of us are well seated (*Ebi te yie*), some are not so well-seated, but others are not well seated at all (*Ebi nte yie koraa*)." The animals gave careful thought to the duiker's remarks, because they had all seen what was happening. They agreed to his suggestion and the meeting was adjourned.

The composer of the song likens the duiker's experience to what happens in life generally: some people are fortunate and live well, while some do not live so well and others do not live well at all. In the free and permissive atmosphere of post-1966 Ghana, which in itself had made possible the public acceptance of this song, there was a more specific interpretation. The new men at the helm of affairs – army and police officers and civilians who as a result of the coup were now the rulers – were well-off (or at least that was how they appeared to the man in the street). They were living well; they were well housed; they rode in big cars. The contrast between the mode of living of the new "ruling class" and that of the ordinary Ghanaian was sharpened by post-coup economic problems with attendant unemployment and hardships, which were now the lot of many people. Such people, like the duiker, were not living well at all.

The song gave currency to phrases and expressions like "Petition please," "point of order," *"Ebi te yie,"* and *"Ebi nte yie."* They were repeated daily by people from all walks of life. To take a concrete example, the expression *"Ebi nte yie"* appeared in an intellectual fortnightly magazine, the *Legon Observer,*[2] as part of a caption to one of a series of satirical articles written by a university professor under the pseudonym "Kontopiaat."

Dancing

Our listing in Chapter 2 of proficiency in dancing among the qualities which a concert party comedian must possess is undoubtedly a clear indication of the important role which dancing plays in comic plays and in Ghanaian society as a whole. It is therefore not surprising that almost all Ghanaian comedians are adept at dances, ranging from traditional dances to current steps in highlife and pop dances.

Comedians are self-trained dancers, just as they are self-tutored actors. Yet they are some of the most proficient dancers known in Ghana. Dancing enters naturally into their acting and it sometimes provides a convenient diversion from a monotonous performance on stage. The dances performed vary from the various Ghanaian traditional ones such as *adowa* and *agbadza,* to modern Ghanaian creations like highlife, *Kpanlogo,* and popular dances from elsewhere such as rock-'n'-roll, cha-cha-cha and the twist. Performed dances will never fail to delight a Ghanaian audience. The plot of a play sometimes revolves around dancing. A suitor is asked to dance for or with the lady he wishes to marry and if she is

Dance, too, plays an integral part in the plays, and here a dancer doing the "Limbo" is being congratulated by the "chief" and his followers.

satisfied, then she agrees to his proposal. Confronted with this requirement, the prospective husband may be expected to exhibit an admirable and extraordinary ability in dancing.

From time to time the dances take acrobatic form. Two comedians, one a female impersonator and the other a young man, begin by exhibiting a wonderful performance of acrobatic dancing. In the process, the "lady" may suddenly jump and fling her legs around the hips of the man and sit there while they both dance. Before or after that, either of them may sit on the floor and dance incredibly well while remaining seated. The "lady" or the man sometimes astounds the audience by lying flat on his back as he dances around.

5
Presentation

The Stage
Because concert parties are itinerant bands, they are very adaptable and can play wherever they find space and an audience. They may play in the courtyard of a village compound on a small platform made of boards or cement or on the stage of a city arts center. No curtains are used. Theirs is a permanently open stage with a dressing corner usually improvized for the show and dismantled when the show is over.

There is generally no sophisticated lighting system. A few electric light bulbs hanging on the stage and providing enough light for the actors to be seen clearly by the audience are all that they require. When there is no electricity, two or three hurricane or "Aladdin" kerosene lamps serve their purpose.

Structure of Performances
Structurally there are four parts to a concert party show. The first of these which lasts for about an hour is the performance of highlife music. It is intended to get the audience settled while giving the music lovers among them their money's worth.

The musical concert is followed by what the actors themselves term "comedies" – a series of short displays or a playlet intended to whet the appetite of the audience for the main play in the program. Two or three of the actors dressed in tight colored long pants and long-sleeved shirts with their faces painted black and their lips, noses, eyebrows painted white hurriedly appear on the stage. Occasionally one or two of them may stuff the front of their shirts with cloths so as to make them look corpulent. They sing and perform fast and extremely complicated dances full of incredible contortions of the pelvis and the trunk of the body which send the audience roaring with laughter.

In presentation, concert party staging strives to recreate the drama of real life –
a king and his court, for example.

Two of them may depart and leave one on the stage to take over
the horseplay and comic activities. He may begin by smoking a
cigarette in a funny manner, putting it at one side of his mouth and
releasing the smoke on the other side. Or he may ingeniously
twist his mouth in such a way as to reverse the cigarette so that the
lighted end of it enters his mouth for about half a minute before he
brings it back in a cloud of smoke.

After this he may laugh in a peculiar manner and move his
mouth and lips in such a way as to provoke laughter from the audience. He may crack a joke, hurl insults at another actor and burst
into prolonged laughter. He may try all sorts of mimicry, simulat-
ing the movement of deformed persons or those of different animals. He may also provoke laughter through sheer use of language, making meaningless or wrong references to everyday
events, places and things.

Sometimes instead of elaborate comedies, a playlet is performed as the second item. Here, for example, is the scenario of
one such playlet performed as a curtain raiser by the Golden Stars
Band. It is entitled "The Priest Who Deserted His God."

The scenario begins with a traditional dance by a group of five,
two women and three men, all dressed in *kente* cloth.

After the dance a Christian minister comes on the stage singing hymns. He is dressed in minister's robes, but hidden underneath these are the costume and body ornaments of a traditional priest. According to his story, he lost his wife and two children, and so he had been thinking of leaving the Christian priesthood to become a "fetish" priest. To provoke laughter, he removes his Christian attire to reveal the "fetish" costume. He dances like a "fetish" priest for a while, and an attendant brings the shrine of the god to the stage. He is ready to start work.

The brothers of a sick person bring him to the priest to be cured. Before prescribing anything, he asks for a hen, six eggs, a bottle of schnapps or gin, and ten cedis. When they bring these he gives them some potion to be drunk by the sick person when they get home.

When a second patient is brought to him, he makes the same demand and prescribes the same cure. He then shares what has been accumulated so far with his attendant. They start helping themselves to drinks.

Unfortunately for them, the two patients die as soon as they drink the medicine given to them by the priest. So while the priest and his attendant are drinking, the kinsmen of the dead patients come to demand back the money and the things that they brought. They have reported the matter to the police. When the priest sees that he is in deep trouble, he regrets that he had left the Christian ministry. He sings hymns of repentance and asks for forgiveness from God.

Thus ends the curtain-raiser which is followed immediately by the third part of the show – the main play of the evening. It is here that the comedians really "go to town" demonstrating their talent as actors, singers, and dancers, and indeed masters of the art of improvization. As an illustration of this we shall again use material staged by the Golden Stars Band. It is entitled "Awoo ne wo yam," literally, "Childbirth Means Your Own Womb." This is to say the child to whom one has given birth is the child one can really call one's own.

Scenario of Main Play

A man comes on to the stage singing about the sad story of his life. He has married thrice, but each marriage has been dissolved at the request of relatives of the wives because he did not have children with any of his spouses. As a result of this he has decided to live all alone in a village.

Realizing that he is drawing near to the end of his life, he has decided formally to give his money and all his property to his nephew Antobam and his niece Faasemkye.

He calls his nephew and niece for the presentation of the gift in the presence of their mother. When he makes the presentation, Faasemkye demands her share for fear that her brother Antobam might use it all before long. Her mother advises her to let Antobam keep the the things, because he is a man. She agrees.

A man comes in singing and lamenting his poverty. He is poor, and on top of that he has no child to care for him or take his place when he dies. Antobam, now rich and married, arrogantly tells the poor man to go and commit suicide. He drives him away.

Faasemkye, having completed a course in sewing, comes to ask Antobam to buy a sewing machine for her, but to her surprise her brother not only refuses but also disowns her. He tells his wife that his sister is the daughter of one of his father's laborers.

Antobam's wife, Abena Grace, fights with Faasemkye. Faasemkye sings, lamenting her lot and receives money from the audience. She goes to report her brother's treatment of her to their mother who comes to find out what really happened, only to be insulted by Antobam and his wife. Antobam's uncle also comes, and Antobam insults him too.

The poor man who was told by Antobam to go and commit suicide falls in love with Faasemkye and marries her. With the help of Faasemkye's uncle, he buys a big farm and becomes rich. He hears a rumor that the police are after Antobam. He comes to tell Antobam, but he pays no heed to him. Faasemkye brings a letter to Antobam who reads from it that he is wanted by the police. Antobam returns, shivering because of the bad news that he has incurred an overdraft of £4,000 at the Ghana Commercial Bank. Alarmed, he begins to sell the clothes he is wearing. He sells everything, excepting his pants. Despite the treatment he gave to his mother, the old lady comes to give him a piece of cloth to wear. Faasemkye now has a baby by her husband, and she brings her in her arms for the naming ceremony. The child is named after three people at once: Faasemkye's uncle, her mother, and her husband. Faasemkye sings happily and seems to like the names of her newborn baby.

A number of morals can be drawn from the story of the play, but what the Golden Stars Band chose to highlight was that the bond between a parent and his or her child cannot be broken. The kindness which Antobam's mother showed to him in his hour of need, despite the treatment he meted out to her, is proof of this.

At the conclusion of the play, the performance is rounded off with another musical concert – the fourth item of the show. The musicians go through their own repertoire of highlife songs composed by their leader and other members of the group. They perform not only those that have been commercially recorded and released to the public but also new ones they want to advertise.

Many shows based on the foregoing structure are performed every weekend in different parts of the country by different concert party bands. Summaries of some other plays are given in the Appendix.

Adaptation

Active interest was shown in concert parties by the Arts Council of Ghana and festivals of concert party plays have been organized. At such festivals a time limit is imposed on the groups which forces them to concentrate only on the main play, leaving out many of the elements which they use to prolong a performance. The Ghana Broadcasting Corporation has also provided program spots for these plays, for example, the Osofo Dadzie television series, an innovation which was most welcome to viewers. However in television presentations, an evening's performance is telescoped into an hour of television time, and the structure of regular performances described above is consequently greatly modified. Specifically the television version omits the musical introduction, the comedies and the concluding music. Moreover the profusion of highlife music which characterizes comic plays is reduced to the barest minimum.

However, as the enthusiastic reponse accorded the festival and television versions of the plays shows, this streamlining of the performance structure does not seem to lessen the enjoyment that the viewing public derives from them, for the actors always manage to incorporate the comic elements that are vital to the tradition and which distinguish their plays from those of other Ghanaian dramatists.

When one looks at the increasing acceptance of the concert party tradition in Ghana and its growing popularity, a number of questions come to mind. What are the factors that have contributed to the popularity of this genre of drama in Ghana? How has it been able to maintain continuity and achieve some growth in its techniques without any form of direct institutional support or guidance?

Role of Talent and Techniques

The concert party tradition has always been practiced by those who look at it as their vocation and who are prepared to devote all their time, thought, and energy to it. They come to it as creative people, or as people who have already developed their peculiar skills and techniques as singers, dancers, guitarists, drummers, or as people with a good command of rhetoric, people whose responses are quick and who already command certain tricks of movement or speech (such as lisping, speaking in dialect or imitating accents).

Because those who come together to form a concert party or join it later are artists, the creative energy that goes into a production is a corporate one. By using the techniques of group play-making, the conception of the play becomes everybody's right from the start. Even when a play starts as the idea of one person, it soon becomes a shared idea which is worked out by all.

In this connection, concert party drama is drama in the oral tradition. In its methods and orientation it is close to traditional practice, particularly as exemplified in storytelling drama. The use of dance, mime, dialogue, and song as avenues of dramatic communication is very much in line with the concept of drama in traditional African societies.

In its choice of modes of communication, concert party drama often falls on the most direct types, those modes that can evoke an immediate response from a large number of people. These include the use of local Ghanaian languages and in particular the main dialects of the Akan language which has the greatest number of speakers as well as others who can follow it; the highlife, which is a widespread form of popular music in Ghana; and comic- or laughter-provoking elements which appeal to all but some of the "highbrow."

Closely connected with the above is the use of techniques of exaggeration and embellishment, techniques also exploited in storytelling drama. The application of these comes out in the kind of statements that are made, in the choice of costume, in movement, in specific acts—particularly those that are familiar or ordinary such as eating, drinking, crying, response to greetings, etc., all of which have features that could be deliberately exaggerated for comic effect. Because of this, a concert party play need not be wholly logical in its construction or wholly credible in its story line. The liberties accorded the storytelling drama apply here also.

But the success of concert party plays is not due to the music, dancing and the humor which form their conspicuous features and the tricks of the trade just indicated. There are a number of contributory sociological, economic and thematic factors. In the remaining three chapters we examine some of these factors in the content analysis, audiences' response and the social functions of the plays.

6
Thematic Sources

Thematically, comic plays reflect several significant Ghanaian social facts and realities. A non-Ghanaian can learn a lot about Ghanaian society by attending comic plays or by reading the stories of the plays. Like popular plays in any society, they are attuned to the interests and experiences of the audiences. The comedians depict or project current social conflicts, problems, and dilemmas which are real to the members of the audience. The numerous social problems which the plays shed light on include the universal conflict of good versus bad; discrimination and ill-treatment meted out by stepmothers, half-sisters, aunts, and housewives to stepchildren, orphans, nieces, nephews, and housemaids; the problems of married life, such as married people not getting along, desertion, and disowning of wives by husbands; evil machinations of men against their fellow men, relatives, or friends; and a host of other social difficulties. Some of these problems are, of course, the obvious concomitants of the rapid social change currently taking place in Ghana and Africa at large.

A common factor of all these plays, and indeed of all concert party plays, is the moral tone which intensely pervades them. They are constructed around various moral issues such as those which we have outlined above. The all-pervading moral element seems to stem from the fact that Ghanaians, like many other African people, are very religious and moralistic. The entire fabric of their social life is based on religion and morality. Social relations and attitudes and behavior are expected to be geared to the integration of the social order. Any deviations from the social norms, values, and standard behavior of the society are considered to be disruptive and to call for correction. Comedians highlight the disruptive tendencies and deviations which are prevalent in Ghanaian society. In that way, they indirectly warn the audience against these tendencies and deviations.

The comedians in effect do two opposite things almost at the same time. They give members of an audience some excitement by dramatizing immoral impulses but at the same time offer them moral lessons, inculcating them with warnings of the dangerous results of not curbing evil tendencies. The ambivalence of the unfolding events in the plays helps members of the audience recognize that such disagreeable impulses are part of mankind's common heritage. They are told, at the same time, that the price of peace is conformity, that it does not pay to violate the values and moral standards of society. This point is forcefully driven home to them by the misery and punishment which, in the end, is always the lot of those who act in violation of the norms and moral expectations of the society.

The ingenious way by which comedians make the issues they highlight in their plays perform this dual function shows their lucid awareness and grasp of the conditions, problems, and conflicts in their social milieu. If one examines some of the situations that really occur in the context of Ghanaian social custom, one will see the way in which common and serious cultural issues are brought into focus by the plays so that their social implications may be considered by the audience.

One issue that forcibly strikes anyone because of its constant recurrence in the plays is the theme of the ill-treatment of orphans and housemaids. Four of the specimen stories in this book (see appendix) take this subject as their theme. The subject deserves close and detailed comparison with the real events reported in newspapers that touch upon the reality of this topic in contemporary Ghana.

In a brief but illuminating article,[1] E. N. Goody shows how common the practice of fostering is in both in northern and southern Ghana. K. A. Busia, the distinguished sociologist and onetime prime minister of Ghana, states in his *Social Survey of Sekondi-Takoradi* that the practice of sending children away to foster parents is common in Ghana. He writes:

> The practice of sending children away to live with relatives and friends is neither new nor uncommon, and in the old days it was a way of ensuring that children receive proper discipline and training from respected members of the community and were not spoilt by over-fond parents. It was also a way in which members

of the extended family shared the responsibility for training their young relatives.[2]

The death of one or both of a child's parents necessitates what Goody terms "crisis fostering" as distinguished from "voluntary fostering."[3] It is the kind of neglect and ill-treatment suffered by orphans who fall into the "crisis fostering" category that is usually brought into relief in the plays; it is the same kind as that suffered by housemaids who very often are, in fact, orphans as well. It must be noted in passing that orphans who lose only one parent are taken care of by the living parent. But if the living parent happens to be the man and he marries again, then the orphans do not often fare any better than those who have lost both parents, as they are often ill-treated by their stepmothers and their half-sisters and brothers. The story of Mansa in this book well illustrates this point.

Indeed, in the very first story in the appendix, an orphaned boy, whose mother on her deathbed has left him in the care of his aunt, suffers ill-treatment and cruel neglect at the hands of the aunt and his cousin. In the second story, Mansa, an orphan girl, is discriminated against and ill-treated by her stepmother and half-sisters. Then again, the story in Synopsis 8 is something like a repetition of Mansa's story. But this time it is a man, Kwame Ataapim, who ill-treats, neglects, and discriminates against his dead brother's daughter, Awura Akua (Lady Akua), while he spoils his own daughters with money and luxury.

A reader who is not familiar with Ghanaian society may be puzzled by the repetition of this theme in concert party plays and wonder whether it is a true reflection of Ghanaian family organization. However, any temptation on his part to reject the idea as mere fiction will surely be restrained by the constant recurrence of themes, a repetition that must to some extent measure the prevalence of the situation in actual daily life.

Perhaps a brief look at the relevant facts from Ghanaian society may be helpful here. Busia's *Social Survey of Sekondi-Takoradi* provides us with empirical evidence on the treatment of housemaids, and we may include orphans in that category. His evidence has since been confirmed by Ioné Acquan in her *Accra Survey*.[4] She asserts that the treatment meted out to housemaids in Accra is similar to that found by Busia in Sekondi-Takoradi. Of a number of case histories of housemaids reported by Busia in his survey, two examples will not only illustrate the sort of inhuman treatment some housemaids received but also how truly concert party plays reflect Ghanaian society in this respect. Here is one case history:

> A married couple, the husband literate, the wife illiterate, have a housemaid, A., a girl 10-years-old. She is related to the husband. A. sleeps in the kitchen, which is full of rats. She used to be allowed a mat and pillow, but because she was a bed-wetter, she was deprived of them, and she now sleeps on a sheet of brown paper and has no pillow. She has two changes of cloth. She does the marketing and assists in cooking, cleaning and washing. She is frequently given corporal punishment. On one occasion, she had red pepper rubbed into her eyes for coming home late from an errand. She begins the day's activities at 5 a.m. and is usually up till after 10 p.m.[5]

How different is this case history from Mansa's life story as revealed in the second story in this book? Such situations are far from rare in Ghanaian society, especially in the towns and cities.

A second case history is even more chilling and reveals some of the gravest ills in Ghanaian family organization:

> B. was a girl 10-years-old, staying with a married couple, the man literate, the woman illiterate. The couple had four children who were left to B.'s care. She also did the marketing and cooking. She had her meals off what was left after the couple and their children had dined. She was provided with two changes of cloth. A short time ago, she became ill, but had to carry on with her duties until she was too weak to do so. No medical attention was sought for her. One afternoon, she fainted, and then the husband sent for some patent medicine from a nearby drug store. The girl died before the medicine was brought.[6]

It is such incredibly inhuman treatment which, when enacted in the plays, arouses spontaneous pity in the audience and sometimes elicits tears. Some members of the audience themselves, their relatives or friends, may have been victims of such ill-treatment and so when it is dramatized on the stage, they find it agonizing and sometimes unbearable. Some shed tears when their own sufferings are, as it were, played back to them.

Another frequently recurring theme is the disowning of wives by their husbands. In the play entitled "The Ungrateful Husband," Ntow disowns his wife after she sustains injuries in a lorry accident.

Are Ghanaian men really so flippant in their marriages as to keep on disowning their wives as the plays seem to indicate? The answer here is that they do not simply disown their wives but rather, like men elsewhere, divorce them to marry other women they consider more fitting. In the traditional face-to-face society, the sanctions of customs and norms exercised more effective control over the individual members of the society and the divorcing of wives could not have been as frequent as it is in the rapidly changing Ghanaian society of today where families are more mobile and some moral values seem to be in a state of flux. The impact of Western education, values and ideas of marriage, quite different from the traditional ones, seems to have increased conflicts between husband and wife, and husbands married under customary law divorce their wives lightly to marry other women. In some cases, a man divorces an illiterate wife to marry a literate one more fitting to his economic and social status as an educated man. Here too Busia provides ample evidence in his survey. He found during his investigations that:

> There were examples of literate men who were first married to illiterate girls under Native Customary law, and later when they were able to afford to marry literate girls under the Ordinance, they divorced their illiterate wives. The practice is not uncommon, and affects marital relationships, as well as the care of children of the first marriage.[7]

The last sentence of this quotation touches in another way a point we have made earlier in this chapter, namely that stepmothers do not always take proper care of their stepchildren. Some stepmothers see to it that their stepchildren do not stay in the same house with their father. If they do, the stepmothers ill-treat them. Some stepfathers ill-treat stepchildren in the same way. This is reflected in the plays.

A third point of interest is that the plays suggest that ordinary Ghanaians still believe in the power of traditional gods, even if this belief is waning gradually under the impact of rapid social change. One concert party story, "God is the Great God," depicts a conflict between the devotees of a god called *kokroko,* led by a chief on one side and some Christians on the other. This conflict, though set in the past rather than the present, seems to provide evidence for prevalence of belief. Further evidence can be found in other stories. One concerns a poor man called Kojo Brake who becomes rich through cocoa farming. His sister, Esi Nana, and his nephew, Kwaku Sharp, resort to juju to kill Kojo Brake in order to take his money. He counteracts their action by consulting a traditional priest who gives him a charm of self-protection. His charm proves more powerful, and so when Kwaku Sharp attempts to kill him with the juju, Sharp becomes mad. The audience accepts this as a normal and just outcome.

7
Comedians And Their Audience

Comedians come from Ghana's rank and file, and therefore the themes of their plays are attuned to the common attitudes and behavior of the ordinary men and women who constitute the greater part of their audience. They know their fellow Ghanaians to be cheerful, happy and somewhat sentimental – especially women. They also know how the ordinary Ghanaian reacts to life's problems and those of other people. They know him in happiness and in distress. They have seen Ghanaian women wailing bitterly at the funeral of a non-relative, thus sharing fully the sorrow of the bereaved family. They know that Ghanaians sometimes spend a whole day or more at the funeral of a friend or a friend's relative to give the friend moral and financial support during his mourning – something considered unnecessary in highly industrialized countries where life is more impersonal and folk are often indifferent to the affairs of others. A Ghanaian in some ways regards his neighbor's calamity as his own and reacts to it in the same way as he would react to his own. It is against such a background that comedians construct and adapt their plays for the stage.

The psychology of the comic play is as simple as the play itself. The comedians frankly state that their primary aim is to make money by entertaining people, and they are conscious of the fact that if playgoers are to continue to pay for the plays, those who attend have to feel that they are getting their money's worth. They also know that Ghanaians, like people the world over, have personal problems such as poverty, bereavement, frustrations, disappointment in love affairs and marriage and so forth. A dramatization of a story mirroring on the stage some of these problems of life, punctuated with songs, jokes, and comical dances can achieve the double purpose of entertaining the audience and at the same time giving them a moral to think about.

In staging the plays, the comedians keep three things at the back of their minds: to give plenty of music to entertain the music lovers among the audience; to amuse and make the audience laugh away their sorrows and worries; and to present some moral in the stories they stage.

Should the response of the audience threaten to interrupt the unfolding narrative of a play, comedians immediately relate to the psychology of the situation. Now and then, some impatient members of the audience may shout suggestions or ideas to an actor or reveal facts as though the protagonist is unaware of them. They are only to be revealed at the appropriate time in the normal course of the play, and a comedian who accepted such hints from the audience and acted according to them would pre-empt the particular scene. When a comedian finds himself in such a situation, he simply ignores the hints and allows the play to proceed normally. The relationship between actor and audience has always been one of the most significant and evocative elements in theatre. To obtain a sense of reality while allowing the audience to retain sufficient disbelief to accept that all is merely an acted tale can be a difficult tightrope to walk, especially when the audience is very young or somewhat unsophisticated. In western critical philosophy, there is the concept of "the willing suspension of disbelief." In Ghana, members of the audience often react to a play by shouting advice or information to the apparently bemused and blissfully ignorant actor.

Such interference usually occurs when an actor enters in the middle of a scene, ignorant of certain facts known to the audience. It may be that somebody is hiding somewhere, or something is hidden, or a fact is temporarily concealed from him only later to be revealed. The following two examples serve to illustrate this point. One tells the story of a rustic farmer who married a sophisticated city lady. During the absence of the farmer, his wife invites a lover into their house and begins to flirt with him, but unfortunately for the woman and her lover, the farmer returns and knocks at the door of the room. With great quickness of mind, the city woman asks her lover to hide under a table which she covers with a large piece of cloth. When the woman lets her husband into the room, he asks her what the covered box is. Her reply is that it is a radio. At this juncture, there can be repeated shouts from the audience, "There is a man hiding under it! She is telling lies"! The farmer pretends that he did not hear the audience and asks his wife to tune the radio for news. He remains in the room until, enchanted by the songs from the "radio box," he lifts it up and, to his surprise, finds a half-naked man under the table. Amidst tremendous laughter from the audience, the would-be lover runs away.

Another example that illustrates the same point occurs in a play in which a pretentious and seemingly clever lady steals her rival's loaf of bread. The rather unassuming woman leaves the house and her box, containing a loaf of bread, in charge of her rival and goes to market to buy food for the household. On her return, she discovers that the loaf of bread is missing from the box. The pretentious woman says she has not seen it. Some members of the audience then shout, "The bread is hidden in her cloth." The actors ignore the shouts and proceed with their performance until one of them asks the woman for a dance and, as she gets up, the loaf of bread falls from her cloth. Her theft is discovered at the appropriate time and, disgraced, she leaves the place in shame.

It is interesting to watch the irritation of some members of an audience at what is happening in a play. They may begin to show disapproval or approval by shouting and booing or in any other way they think fit. In one play, a sister and a friend of Agnes, the heroine, attempt to persuade her to break her marriage and accompany them to Takoradi to lead the life of a harlot. They tell her she has much to gain by leading that kind of life. She not only refuses to follow their advice but also denounces the harlot's life. Her action is very much approved by members of the audience and they frequently show their approval by applause and by presenting her with gifts of money.

This brings us to the general technique by which comedians induce an audience to present them with gifts of money. They earn these special tips by appealing to the audience's emotions as well as to their moral judgment. Besides the general admission fee, the actors seek to earn individual gifts of money by their performances. From the beginning of a play, they gradually arouse the feelings of the audience. They sing a carefully timed series of apposite songs to drive home what they have been trying to convey by words and action. Through the medium of songs, which often convey messages or ideas faster than dialogue, comedians moralize the incidents in the play. They may bemoan the lot of orphans, deserted or disowned wives or husbands, and poverty-stricken or childless persons. They may extol virtues or condemn vices displayed in the story being dramatized. The feelings of the audience

Ghanaians attach much importance to clothes, and actors are able to provide comic relief by dressing in foolish apparel.

are worked on until they reach a climax with a series of songs, and the desired results are achieved. Besides the usual applause that greets a success, some members of the audience spontaneously walk up to the stage and present actors with gifts of money. The spontaneity with which they do this seems to be an indication of the effectiveness of the actors' technique.

Similarly, comedians occasionally arouse competitive feeling between men in the audience on one side and women on the other. A female impersonator may sing a song full of imputations about the character of Ghanaian men. This will induce women in the audience to offer "her" money. In reply, a comedian, representing men, will sing a song full of even more damaging imputations against the character of modern Ghanaian women and in that way impel men among the audience to feel that they, too, should shout and give money. Having thus aroused a competitive feeling among the audience, actors continue with a further interchange of imputations thus infusing some sort of collective excitement among the sexes, thereby obtaining money from both groups.

Although acting is an art, actors expect some reward for their efforts. Indeed the acting of Ghanaian comedians is particularly geared to the financial motive, for their parties depend for their immediate survival on donations received. It is not for nothing that they sing specially chosen songs which are filled with African grief-soothing philosophies. Nor is it for nothing that parts of the plays are made to appeal to the common sentiments and ardent emotions of an audience. Comic plays are not unique in this determination to aim for common sympathy. All successful popular plays tend to draw on eternal and deep human emotions no matter in what language they may be played. There is thus a dual effect upon the audience. The comedians entertain by appealing to the sense of humor but they achieve their financial objectives best by playing upon the emotions.

8
Audience Response

The themes of the plays which are in effect mirror images of everyday life experiences, current social problems, conflicts, and dilemmas cannot but evoke active and expressive responses from typical African audiences like those of Ghanaian comic plays. Ghanaian audiences are always actively and intensely involved in the unfolding episodes of the plays. They laugh, applaud, and show sympathetic feelings according to what happens in a play. In short, they give visible expression to their feelings at a play's various stages. Because of this, it is necessary to consider the audience when one is discussing these plays, for even more than most theatre, Ghanaian comic plays derive their effects from the reinforcements they receive from their eager viewers.

As indicated above, one practical way in which members of the audience express their feelings and emotions is by walking onto the stage, sometimes in a procession, to offer money to actors in appreciation of the performance. They are motivated by many reasons when they offer gifts of money.

Some of them offer the gifts purely because of the quality of the actors' performances. For instance, a guitarist may play a lovely piece of music, and men, women, boys, and girls in the audience will present him with money. Here, they respond mainly to the beauty of the music played. Similarly, in accordance with Ghanaian custom, a member of the audience, usually a woman, may walk onto the stage to congratulate an actor by waving a handkerchief or part of her cloth over the actor's head. Conversely, she may go onto the stage to tease an actor. A comedian acting the part of a wicked husband who has disowned or maltreated his wife and who has accumulated many debts may be disgraced in the end by being undressed publicly by his creditor. Women in the audience, in reacting to his situation, may tease the

68

Everyone in this packed house is riveted by the goings-on on the stage.

husband by pointing to his nakedness. They may tell him publicly that it is his wickedness which has landed him in this miserable condition.

Some members of the audience who agree with what an actor says may present him with money. A comedian acting the part of a man who has been fooled or duped by a woman may make a re- mark or sing a song pointing out and condemning a general defect in women's character evidenced by his bitter experience. Some men in the audience who from their own experience have formed the same opinion about women may present money to the actor who seems to be voicing their views on the stage. Similarly, an actor playing the part of a wronged woman may sing a song or make a comment on an evil trait in the character of men. This will receive a spontaneous response from women in the audience who will demonstrate their agreement with money gifts.

Humane feeling and sympathy for the role of a person whose part a comedian is acting may also prompt people to offer him gifts. An orphan who is being maltreated by her aunt and her cousins, or a stepmother and her half-sisters, and thus enduring the worst conditions in life, may sing a series of songs bemoaning the fate of orphans and people who have lost all their relations. The words of songs sometimes elicit not only sympathetic feeling and kind gestures, but even tears from some members of the audience. The numerous songs that punctuate a comic play generally philosophize on the problems of life and console men who find themselves in similar situations. The words of such songs in one way or another remind playgoers of similar or comparable incidents in their lives. The relief they get from the solace offered by the philosophy embodied in a song may prompt them to give money to the singers.

From time to time, members of the audience reply to statements made by the comedians with which they disagree or which contravenes accepted Ghanaian social principle. For example, Ghanaians believe that every man or woman should marry, live an organized family life, and raise and care for children. Thus, in the course of a play, if a player acting the part of a woman declares that "she" will not marry and have children because there is no point in having children and that it is better to live a happy-go-lucky life enjoying a "good time" and amassing wealth and clothes, her statement will immediately be met with protesting shouts from women in the audience. They will ask her to bear in mind the days of her old age when she will need the services of children or grandchildren.

On the other hand, if a comedian acting the part of an extravagant man who spends lavishly and senselessly on "good time" girls, justifies his actions by maintaining that that is how a man should live, some men among the audience will promptly condemn him as a fool.

Examples of these responses can be discovered readily by personal observation. The writer attended a comic play at Kpandu in the Volta Region. In one of the "scenes," a man, infatuated by the beauty of a certain woman, told her that he had no wife, whereas in actual fact he had one. He started flirting with the woman and when his wife, now pregnant, arrived at the house, he drove her away telling her that he did not know her. The poor woman burst into tears. Observing the scene, a woman friend who accompanied the writer turned to him and remarked, "You see, you men are not good." Later conversation revealed that she had had a somewhat similar experience. Her boyfriend had once made love to her own girlfriend and this had brought their friendship to an end.

In a scene from another comic play, a cocoa farmer who had been toiling on his farm all his life with his wife and children, dies just at the time he is about to enjoy the fruits of his labor. The farmer's maternal nephew who inherited the estate from him maltreats the widow and her children. He drives them away from the farmer's house, refusing to care for them. He does not even give them money for food. A man in the audience, witnessing some of the demerits of nephew-inheritance dramatized on the stage, said in the hearing of the writer and other people near him, "This nephew-inheritance must be stopped."

In the course of the same scene, tears were seen flowing down the cheeks of a girl in the audience. When asked why she was crying, she replied that she was sorry for the widow and her children. She further revealed that similar treatment was once meted out to her sister when her sister's husband died.

A similar response was given in a comic play staged at Saltpond, a coastal town in the Central Region. One section of the play showed a woman who had sustained injuries in a lorry accident. She had bandages all over her body and, unable to walk, had to crawl on her knees towards her husband. He started driving the injured wife away, telling another woman who was with him that he did not know the mad woman crawling toward him. As the injured wife began weeping, singing, and bemoaning her fate, many members of the audience literally queued up to present her with money. The writer was sitting on a seat between two women. The woman sitting on the left of the writer was weeping bitterly and the one on the right turned to her and said, "Compare this with your case and console yourself." The remark from her friend made her weep all the more.

Psychologists might maintain that the woman who wept bitterly in response to somebody else's misfortune released her feeling of grief which otherwise would have remained buried in her. This makes for a variant on the classic concept of catharsis. She went home from the playhouse psychologically better than she was before attending the play. The emotional healing of the injury which her agonizing experience had caused began that night. The same thing can be said of members of the audience who give uninhibited expression of their feelings and emotions at comic plays. The plays offer them potent medicine and balm for their psychological wounds.

On another occasion, a woman who was watching a comic play and laughing suddenly began to shed tears at a touching scene in the play. When she was asked at the end of the play why she was shedding tears, she said she was so much touched by that particular aspect of the play that she could not help but weep. She asked the writer, "Didn't you see many people weeping?"

Her reaction touches on the phenomenon of suggestion which operates among the audience of a comic play. Probably the woman saw other members of the audience shedding tears in response to a touching incident and she did the same. Similarly, the presentation of money to actors whose performances rouse the emotional feelings of an audience may be partly due to suggestion. A member of the audience sees people offering money to an actor and does the same.

It is difficult, however, to know whether the response of a person is spontaneous or due to suggestion. The only situation in which one can be perfectly sure direct suggestion is operating is when an actor asks the audience to do something, for example, to join in a song or to laugh or hoot at another actor, and the audience does so. Nevertheless, we can safely assume that indirect suggestion does operate on the audience during comic plays. There is a constant and more often than not a successful attempt on the part of actors to play on audience emotions and feelings which makes them highly suggestible.

The example of the responses described above may give readers the impression that it is mostly women who give overt or visible expressions to their feelings while watching comic plays. Men too behave similarly, but they do not shed tears because, according to Ghanaian custom, it is considered unmanly to do so.

Occasionally members of an audience attend plays to be observed rather than to observe. For them, the play provides the occasion for a personal display. In the course of a comic play a man from the audience may stand up in front of the stage or walk right onto the stage and dance with the actors. He may do this more than once and sport a queer-looking hat or smoke an extraordinary pipe. In this way, he gets great delight from all the attention he gains. Even women do this. During the writer's attendance at comic plays at Saltpond, he noted two particular girls who always went to the stage several times to present money to actors. It seemed probable that they were enjoying the opportunity provided by the play to show themselves off.

If these expressive and, in some instances, therapeutic audience responses to comic plays do not point to all the social functions of the plays, they at least constitute eloquent indicators of some sociological and psychological needs that they fulfill.

9
The Social Functions Of Plays

The socio-psychological needs that comic plays fulfill and other social functions they perform are manifold, and this is because comic plays may be looked at from a number of perspectives. They may be looked at purely as drama with attention to such aspects as plot, mode of presentation, and audience response. They may be looked at as musical entertainments and a musicologist can study the type of music used in the performances. A historian may examine their origin and diffusion in Ghana and beyond. A sociologist may analyze their influence on people's attitude, behavior, and social relationships. As it must have been evident to the reader by now, the perspective of the writer is sociological, but, where necessary, he has adopted a multidisciplinary approach to take care of the multi-faceted nature of the subject.

Since comic plays constitute a social activity to which all Ghanaians respond with enjoyment, they naturally exert influence on the thoughts, values, and attitudes of the audience. This is true if we also argue that plays reciprocate these same values by mirroring the assumptions of the audience as they already exist as mores prior to the drama. The influence may be functional and is probably dysfunctional as well. The social functions of plays are considered in detail below.

It may be necessary to clarify the meaning of the concept of function as used in this study. It is used here in the familiar sociological and anthropological sense where the social functions of any social institution, usage, or activity – be it the family, religion, the punishment of a crime, or a funeral celebration – "is the contribution it makes to the continuity of the social structure"[1] in which it is found. Lapiere and Farnsworth give a useful definition of the function of a social institution which embodies the idea just quoted: they state that it "is the guidance of the individual into

modes of behavior that assist one way or another in the maintenance of group life."[2] Thus the social function of comic plays is the
contribution they make to the maintenance of the process of
Ghanaian social life. Conversely, the social dysfunction of the
plays, if any, is how their influence detracts from or militates
against the integration and effectiveness of Ghanaian social life.

If the dysfunctional influence of comic plays were demonstra-
ble, a more realistic procedure in a study like this would be to pre-
cede the analysis of their social functions with their dysfunctions.
However, it will be extremely difficult, if not impossible, to
demonstrate by scientific method how the influence of the plays
militates against the social life of Ghanaians.

If we impute any dysfunctional influences to the plays on account of what we see on the stage, we shall cease to be objective
and scientific and join a band of moralists and reformists who, for
example, ardently maintain that the cinema exerts "bad" socializ-
ing influence on children. But the wrong assumptions of such
moralists and reformists have been convincingly exposed by psychologists such as Lapiere and Farnsworth who rightly point out
that the effects of any thing which people see depend on their past
experience. They stress that "the sex-laden motion picture can be
of no certain and consistent effect upon the children or the adults
who see it. To most, young and old, it will probably be just two
hours of pleasant relaxation; to some it will perhaps be only the
first picture of a double bill; to the critics it may be 'B' picture; and
to the young lovers it may be nothing but an opportunity for
holding hands."[3]

It appears, therefore, that there is no method short of intuition
by which we can ascertain the dysfunctions of comic plays. But,
however desirable a quality intuition may be for a poet, it is not
something to be trusted too far by a scientist, natural or social.
With this limitation, it looks as if we cannot do otherwise than ignore the possible but unknown dysfunctions of the plays and
analyze their social functions for which we seem to have observ-
able evidence from the responses of the members of the audience
to the play as described at length in this book.

Let us now return to the concept of "function." Two aspects of it
are germane to our analysis and it seems necessary to explain
them first. They are manifest and latent functions.[4] In sociological
analysis the manifest function of any social institution or custom
is the intended and easily recognizable contribution it makes to

the maintenance of the social order. In other words, it is the intended and obvious ways in which it serves some social need. The latent function, on the other hand, is its concealed, not-so-obvious, and unintended consequences which also help in maintaining the social system. Applying these definitions to our analysis, the manifest social functions of comic plays are the employment they provide for comedians and the entertainment and recreation they provide for playgoers. The latent social functions of the plays which will be discussed in detail in this chapter are the incidental and not-so-obvious need they serve in Ghanaian society.

Manifest Functions

Concert party plays are designed for the entertainment of an audience which stands in different social relationship to the performers from what we normally find in traditional society. While traditional recreational bands perform as a service, a tribute to an individual or for their own enjoyment and the enjoyment of the members of their communities that may come to watch them, concert parties do not perform for themselves but for an audience that pays to watch them. Hence the intensity of economic consideration varies greatly between the two types of performers. It is quite low among traditional bands but very high among concert party bands, since they depend on this for their living. Hence making plays that will appeal to the ordinary run of audience becomes a primary motivation. For the same reason repeating materials and techniques that have proved successful becomes an important stabilizing factor in their modes of operation. Deviations from standard or proven forms may be attempted if these would heighten the appeal of the plays which, as we have seen, lies in the presentation of the comic, exhibition of dance skills, and use of humor rather than intricate production techniques or experiments in dramatic form.

Because of this, the establishment of a performer-audience chain before, during, and after a performance becomes important. This chain is established in the first instance through advertisement. Since a concert party is an itinerant group, its visit becomes an important news item and may cause a stir in a small community. Certain expectations are raised which may be heightened by the form of pre-show local advertisement that is used for drawing the audience to the show.

Many bands have developed techniques for this and are in this respect differentiated from traditional groups. Indeed the need for proper promotion of shows has encouraged the development of a business side to the organization of concert parties, and quite a few of them have their own managers and local agents.

The second mode of establishing the performer-audience chain is through the preliminary musical concert. During the course of performance, the chain is sustained through the encouragement of various forms of audience participation and responses. The musical concert that ends the performance has a similar function, for a different level of identification is established between performer and audience when the actor, made up and disguised, changes and comes back on to the stage to pick up his guitar and sing.

The performer-audience chain also makes it easy for comic plays to be used sometimes as a medium for public information campaigns, whether they are designed to persuade the public to help in national development or to be law-abiding. Bob Cole, the famous comedian, claims to have been specifically instructed to do this. He made sure that he passed on some information to the audience at the end of the play he performed. At the end of one play performed in 1965 he reminded the audience of the great work being done by the government of that time in the form of development projects and stressed that the government needed their support to be able to carry out the projects. On another occasion, he ascribed the high death rate among young men to the evil habit of narcotics. He cited the example of a young student who went mad as a result of smoking Indian hemp and called the audience's attention to the plight of many young men then in the mental hospital, all as a result of such dangerous habits. He exhorted all members of the audience not to smoke Indian hemp because it shortens a person's life. There is no doubt that at least some members of the audience after hearing him became scared of smoking Indian hemp and to that extent the advice and warning contributed to the system of social control.

Comic plays are also sometimes manifestly used to portray special aspects of Ghanaian culture. In conjunction with the restoration of African independence and the desire to show the world that Ghana had its own distinctive and rich culture, comedians made conscious efforts to introduce many items of Ghanaian culture into their plays. If death occurs in a play, a Ghanaian funeral celebration is staged, with all the people wearing current mourning clothes. There are appropriate drumming and dancing, drinks are served, donations given, and all the other main features of Ghanaian funeral celebrations are dramatized.

The traditional priest, the man who held and still holds an important place in traditional Ghanaian society, is sometimes introduced into the play. He comes in full regalia to dance and to be consulted by people in need of divination.

Although concert parties visit both cities and towns, it must be noted that their art is, strictly speaking, an urban-oriented art. In urban centers, where traditional bands are disappearing, they provide the only form of live entertainment available to people. This cannot but assure them a place in social life.

Because concert parties are urban phenomena, they also have some attraction for non-urban communities. When they go to small towns, they provide a different sort of entertainment from what the inhabitants normally have. Hence even where there are traditional recreational bands and storytelling groups, the occasional visit of a concert party band is welcomed as a change. Obviously for economic reasons, the itinerary of concert parties avoids villages except where there are clusters of villages that are close enough to one another for audiences to be drawn to a performance in one of them.

Latent Functions of the Plays

Whether plays are performed in urban or rural areas, there are certain psychological needs that they seem to fulfill and which, therefore, encourage individuals to come and see the play. Emotional tensions and stresses are always present in human life, and playgoers have their share of them.

When these are unreleased, a person becomes withdrawn, timid, aggressive, and irritable. Continuous emotional stress may wear him or her out. It may even lead to nervous breakdown and insanity in extreme cases. Thus continuous emotional tensions and stresses are not only harmful to an individual's personality, but they may affect attitudes and behavior and have a disruptive influence on social relationships.

Any activity that enables its participants to release their emotional tensions fulfills these psychological needs and is therefore functional to the social system of the participants. Comic plays enable members of the audience, through their active responses

So realistic is the acting that members of the audience proceed to the stage to give money when actors ask for it or when they have given an affecting performance.

Concert party announcement in a recent *People's Daily Graphic*.

to the plays such as laughing, walking on to the stage to offer actors money, and shedding tears (especially by women), to release their emotional tensions and stresses.

Out of 885 respondents interviewed in a survey of people attending comic plays, 529 claimed to have seen somebody shedding tears while watching performances. Out of the total respondents, 199, a majority of whom were women, admitted that they had themselves shed tears. Audiences are presented with echoes of their own bitter or happy human relationships and experience or those of their friends, and they get the opportunity to purge themselves of their grief which their sad experience caused them or to relive their happy experiences as the case may be.

The operative expressions "Ebi te yie " and "Ebi nte yie" in the African Brothers song which we described in Chapter 4 serve as a safety valve for the releasing of tensions. People who lost their jobs in the wave of the heavy unemployment that swept over Ghana at the time and were therefore enduring the demoralizing conditions of the jobless, shouted them out at the rich and well-living members of society. When they saw their "social betters" riding in Mercedes Benz, one of them would shout "Ebi te yie, " and another would respond "Ebi nte yie." In doing so, they released some of the emotional tensions created by their condition and felt better for it. One can hurl the expression "Ebi te yie" at any person or group of persons better off than oneself. The expressions in the song facilitate this sort of envious teasing, which goes on at all levels of Ghanaian society.

In addition, there are several values in Ghanaian society which plays reinforce as well as serving as emotional safety valves for playgoers. For example, the kinship system or the extended family system is important to Ghanaians. This is not only because the members inherit from each other, but also because they owe it as a duty to help each other in time of need and illness. The extended family system serves as a social security. In traditional Ghanaian society, custom demands that the kinsfolk of a dead relative take good care of his children just as they would take care of their own children. Any relative who shirks this responsibility or ill-treats the orphans of a dead relative invites misfortunes and illness (meted out by the dead relative). However, as a result of social change, the collective responsibility of the extended family system is breaking down. The children of dead relatives are in some instances neglected because guardians are not fulfilling their customary obligations.

When this type of neglect is enacted in the plays, a relative who has failed to discharge his obligations to the child or children of a dead relative is always shown in a terrible condition. In the play he is afflicted with sudden illness. This serves as a warning to people in the audience who are guilty of this, while those who are victims of neglect may rejoice in seeing the fate of their cruel kinsmen.

It is thus the manifest functions – economic, entertainment, and recreation – as well as the latent functions – moral and psychological – that have led to the establishment and popularity of the concert party tradition in Ghana. There is evidence that this tradition will continue to flourish, for concert party artists are on the side of both tradition and innovation.

APPENDIX
Eight Ghanaian Concert Parties
(Synopses)

Below are synopses of eight Ghanaian concert party plays, collected by the author during his fieldwork in Ghana. They represent the rich variety of themes present in concert parties. Presented as comedies with musical entertainment, each play also concludes on a moral note. The plays were given in Twi or Fante, and sometimes in both languages, since they are mutually intelligible, depending on the mother tongue of the actors.

Synopsis 1
TITLE: The Death of One's Mother Deprives One
of One's Family Ties
ORIGINAL TITLE: Woni wu a na wabasua asa
ORIGINAL LANGUAGE: Twi
PRODUCTION: Ahamano's Band

One of two sisters dies. On her deathbed, she leaves her son in the care of her sister, who has a daughter of her own named Felicia. She pampers the daughter by lavishing all her money on her and refuses to give even a pesewa to her dead sister's son, now an orphan.

On his own initiative, the orphan apprentices himself to a trade, and by dint of hard work he qualifies. He then has to pay some money to his master for the tutorship, and so he goes to his aunt for help. She refuses to give him anything and drives him away with insults. Instead, she gives all her money to her own daughter who wastes it like the Prodigal Son. The girl in turn gives the money to her boyfriend, thus reversing the custom that requires the boyfriend to provide the girlfriend with money.

The orphan prays to his dead mother and the gods for help, and his aunt suddenly falls ill. Felicia, the "Prodigal Daughter," calls in a Muslim to cure her mother. Being a soothsayer, the Muslim sees that the woman's illness is due to the ill-treatment of her late sister's son. Hearing this, Felicia pleads with the Muslim to help her. He cures the sick woman and warns her against any further ill-treatment of the orphan. Felicia urges her mother, after she has recovered, to help her cousin, but the mother pays no heed to her entreaties and instead becomes more infuriated and attempts to drive Felicia away for pleading for her cousin. Felicia then collects money from her mother and departs. The orphan returns to make a second bid for money to pay the tutor, but once again the aunt refuses to give him anything. She also insults him. Enraged, the orphan wants to fight his aunt but he restrains himself. He prays again to the ghost of his dead mother and to the gods to avenge his ill-treatment. Without any money to buy a drink, he pours a libation of water. His prayer is heard by those to whom he prays, and the ghost of his mother comes in the night to the aunt, hits her, and she falls seriously ill.

Felicia returns from her outing to find her mother seriously ill and lying almost dead on the floor. She shouts for help, but her friends will not offer any. Felicia calls her cousin, whom she now describes as a madman – an idea she picked up from her mother – and the Muslim. When the orphan arrives, the Muslim asks him whether he should cure the wicked aunt. He hesitates in giving an answer, but Felicia entreats him to allow her mother to be cured. After the mother is cured, she is informed of what has happened. She regrets her behavior and apologizes to the nephew, giving him a cloth to wear in place of the shabby clothes he is dressed in. Felicia too apologizes and gives her cousin money. The orphan happily adorns his new cloth, and the play ends with everyone happy.

Moral: The title of the play suggests its moral, and the action bears out the ill-treatment that an orphan can receive from an aunt and a cousin. What happens to the aunt is thus a warning to people who maltreat the children of dead relations.

Synopsis 2
TITLE: Treat Somebody's Child As Your Own
ORIGINAL TITLE: Ye wo yonko ba se wo ba
ORIGINAL LANGUAGE: Fante
PRODUCTION: Kakaiku's Band

(The story of Cinderella adapted and given an African background.) An elderly Asante man who is farming at Fanti Nyaka-mase goes to Kumasi for the weekend. In a mood for fun, he decides to go to a nightclub called Jamboree where he meets a Fanti woman named Nkatiaba. He marries her, and they have two daughters. By his first wife, who has died, he has another daughter named Mansa, who is a young girl. The new mother, however, discriminates between her own daughters and Mansa, giving nice clothes to them while Mansa is required to wear a single shabby cloth all the time. Mansa does all the household chores, including cooking, while her two sisters are left free to enjoy themselves.

On one occasion, when the two beloved daughters are having a good time with a boyfriend, Mansa goes to consult them about the food she is preparing. Later they accuse her of misbehaving with the boyfriend, and Mansa is scolded and beaten by her stepmother. After cooking the food, she takes it to Nkatiaba, the stepmother, who then gives it to her daughters while sending Mansa back to the kitchen to sweep the floor before being allowed to eat. When she finishes that task, Mansa finds that her sisters have eaten most of the food and then had poured water into what Nkatiaba had left for Mansa to eat. When she discovers this, Mansa weeps bitterly, singing pitiful songs.

In another scene, Nkatiaba reveals to her own daughters for the first time the fact that Mansa is not her own flesh and blood but rather the daughter of a previous wife. Haughtily, the daughters tell this to Mansa, and she realizes why she is singled out for maltreatment.

Meanwhile, Nkatiaba's husband falls ill, and Mansa alone cares for him. He dies, and when Mansa comes to tell the news to her stepmother and sisters, Nkatiaba asks Mansa to stay at home to look after the house while she and her daughters go visit the dead father. For the funeral celebration, Nkatiaba buys mourning cloth for each of her daughters but none for Mansa. Because there would be many people at the celebration, Mansa pleads with Nkatiaba for a new cloth, but she is refused. Mansa weeps throughout the funeral, wearing her shabby clothes while her sisters are adorned in beautiful new mourning cloths.

Not long afterward, the chief of the town in which the now-widowed Nkatiaba lives, beats a gong-gong for all the people to assemble in his palace to celebrate his annual festival. The question of clothes arises again. Nkatiaba secretly buys two sets of cloths for her daughters and advises them not to tell Mansa, to whom she did not give any. She pretends that she and Mansa will not attend the festival. But Mansa comes from the kitchen and sees her two sisters holding their clothes and discussing how they will attend the festival in the chief's palace the next day. She joins the discussion and fondly examines the two cloths. Later, in the night, she weeps bitterly and calls on her dead mother to come and see her pitiful situation and, if possible, take her away.

In the night, while Mansa is sleeping, the ghost of her mother appears with beautiful clothes and shoes and a lady's umbrella so that Mansa can attend the chief's festival the next day. The ghost embraces the sleeping daughter, bemoaning her condition, and departs. Mansa, dreaming, wakes up, but her mother's ghost disappears before she is fully awake. Mansa is sorry that her mother has not taken her away, but she is overjoyed by the beautiful presents.

The day of the festival comes. Mansa's sisters dress in their new clothes and go to the festival, leaving Mansa in the kitchen. When they have left, Mansa dresses herself gorgeously, and when she gets to the festival, she is radiant among the crowd assembled there. The chief sits in state, and ladies dance to the festival drumming. Mansa joins them and is unrecognized by her sisters. Then, during the dance, realizing that she must be home before her sisters, she steals away. The chief is disturbed when he no longer sees the lady whose beauty had infatuated him. Annoyed, he disperses the gathering and sends people to find the lady. But she is nowhere to be found. Fortunately for him, in her anxiety to escape before her absence would be noted, Mansa leaves one of her shoes in the palace. The chief finds it and immediately recognizes it as belonging to the beautiful young lady. His chances of finding the lady now become bright.

The chief orders the gong-gong to be beaten for all the women who attended the dance to assemble at the palace. Each of them is asked in turn to put on the shoe; the woman whose foot fitted into the shoe would obviously be the owner and thus become the chief's lady. All the women try on the shoe, including Mansa's sisters, but it fits none of them. After a thorough search, Mansa, wearing her shabby cloth, is brought from the kitchen. She is asked to try it on, and to the surprise of everyone, including the sisters, it fits her perfectly. Upon persuasion, Mansa admits the shoe is hers and that she is the lady who had danced before the chief. She is asked to go dress herself in the clothes she had worn to the festival, and when she returns, now gorgeously attired, she tells the whole story to the chief and all assembled. Hearing it, the chief wants to banish Nkatiaba from his district. Mansa pleads for forgiveness in vain. The chief then marries Mansa, and the two sisters, whom she had served from infancy, now become her maidservants. The chief and Mansa celebrate their marriage with music and dancing.

Moral: Stepmothers should treat their stepchildren as their own. If they maltreat the stepchildren, God in mysterious ways punishes them for their wickedness.

SYNOPSIS 3
TITLE: The Taxi Driver and the Wicked Friend
ORIGINAL LANGUAGE: Twi
PRODUCTION: Onyina's Band

A young lady called Serwa is married to an unemployed driver named Bob. She secures work for him from the owner of a newly-bought taxi, and Bob is hired as a driver. When he leaves for work, two of his friends—Mambo and the Boy Skido—visit the house looking for him. They ask Serwa to tell Bob to meet them at their usual rendezvous. Serwa delivers this message to Bob when he returns from work, and Bob goes off to meet his friends for a drink. Bob has now adopted a slogan: "The more you get, the more you spend."

The owner of the taxi, having learned of Bob's drinking habits, warns him strongly against drinking. Despite repeated warnings, Bob gets drunk, and the taxi owner therefore goes to collect the car keys from him, meaning that he is dismissed. Serwa pleads for her husband, and the taxi owner agrees to let Bob continue working.

But Bob does not learn his lesson, and he and his friends go drinking again. The taxi owner is thus obliged to dismiss Bob, and he collects the car keys from him. Now unemployed again, Bob becomes as poor as his friends, and they are reduced to drinking palm wine.

During one of their drinking bouts, Bob's two friends steal two pounds from a palm wine seller and hide it in Bob's coat. A policeman is called in, and Bob is arrested. Bob now appears in prisoner's clothes, followed by a policeman. The Boy Skido makes fun of Bob's condition. Serwa and Bob's sister now ask the Boy Skido for money to pay Bob's fine so that he can be released from prison. The Boy Skido will only give the money on condition that Serwa marry him. This she refuses to do, and he refuses to give her the money. So while Bob, dressed in a prison uniform, is working under the supervision of a stern policeman, and Serwa and Bob's sister are weeping, the Boy Skido continues to laugh at him and tease him.

When Serwa appeals against the conviction of her husband, Bob's sentence is quashed, and he rejoins his wife and sister.

Bob's wicked friends are later arrested when it became known that they were the people who had stolen the palm wine seller's money. Fortune smiles on Bob again. Released from prison, he is invited to succeed his uncle as chief of Mampong (a town north of Kumasi). He is installed as chief and goes to visit people with whom he had stayed while he was a taxi driver. When the Boy Skido and Mambo are released from prison, after serving their sentence, they go to Mampong to greet Bob. Serwa asks Mambo to live with them in the palace. There is merrymaking, and everyone, including the chief, dances. Afterward, the linguist ("spokesman") of the chief gives the moral of the play.

Moral: Having too many friends can get you in trouble. God always saves the innocent, however much the suffering may be. Be as kind to your detractors and enemies as Serwa was to Mambo.

SYNOPSIS 4
TITLE: It is Good to Have Children
ORIGINAL TITLE: Awo ye
ORIGINAL LANGUAGE: Twi
PRODUCTION: Apiakubi's Band

An unemployed clerk named Mr. Johnson becomes rich overnight by winning the first prize of £5,000 from the Ghana National Lottery. He meets an attractive woman named Amponsah, with whom he flirts for some time. When Amponsah's parents hear that their daughter is living with Mr. Johnson, they come to his house to take her away. Mr. Johnson tells them that he plans to marry her, so he and the parents come to terms. They demand a brideprice and other gifts, and Mr. Johnson, much in love with Amponsah, gives them everything they ask. Satisfied with his love for their daughter, the parents agree to the marriage and give most of the things they demanded back to the bridegroom. Thus Mr. Johnson and Amponsah continue to live together.

Mr. Johnson's niece comes to stay with the couple as maidservant, and Mr. Johnson employs a Yoruba houseboy. His grandfather, aunt, and uncle, having heard of his new wealth, also come to visit and demand large sums of money from him.

Mr. Johnson buys a sewing machine for his niece, and Amponsah, now expecting the baby she has so longed for, asks him to buy a sewing machine for her, too. Mr. Johnson advises her to wait until after the birth of the child, but she disagrees and a quarrel ensues. Amponsah's parents soon hear that their daughter is being ill-treated, and they come to take her away from Mr. Johnson — who, having squandered his money, is now poor. His clothes wear out, and in tattered rags, he now approaches the relatives who had once approached him for money. At first, they think he is a madman and when they recognize him, they decide he is a disgrace to the extended family. They cancel his name from the family book and send him away. Mr. Johnson now sings, bemoaning his lot.

Meanwhile, Amponsah, now divorced, gives birth to a girl. But Amponsah soon thereafter dies, and the father being not at home, the daughter becomes a "good-time" girl, wandering from place to place. During her wanderings, she happens to meet a poor, shabbily dressed man who is Fanti, a member of her father's tribe. She tells the story of her life to him, how she had lost her mother and had never seen her father. She gives him the name and description of her father as it had been disclosed to her by certain people. The shabbily dressed man turns out to be Mr. Johnson, and he reveals his identity to her. Daughter and father become reunited, and the daughter buys new clothes for him.

Seeing Mr. Johnson dressed so, his relatives now think he has become rich again, and they come visit him to ask for money. They bring out the family book and start to rewrite his name in it. But Mr. Johnson and his daughter decide to rough them up, and they flee, leaving their clothes behind.

Moral: Men should take good care of their wives when they marry and not rely on their relatives at the expense of the wives in case their relatives throw them out when they become poor. They should also look after their children, since they may have to rescue their fathers from poverty and disgrace.

SYNOPSIS 5
TITLE: Man is Ungrateful
ORIGINAL LANGUAGE: Twi
PRODUCTION: E. K. Nyame's Band

A noble-looking woman desiring a child consents to marry an educated but poor farmer. With her money, he leaves her in town and goes to his village with his workers to tend his cocoa farm. Within a short period of time, the farm produces an abundant crop, which the farmer harvests and sells for a large sum of money. Now rich, he decides to return to the town and stay with his wife. After the couple have enjoyed themselves for several days, the wife asks permission to visit kinsmen in another town. No sooner does she depart than the husband begins to receive visits from all types of women. Soon he is having a good time with them — drinking, singing, and dancing. His money begins to dwindle. One of his workers hears that the wife, who is his mistress, is unwell, and he comes to his master to tell him. The husband, who has told his women visitors that he is unmarried, pretends that he doesn't understand the worker. All the worker's attempts to explain the situation are drowned out by the master's shoutings, and he finally gives up and goes away.

The wife, now stricken by blindness, comes to ask her husband for money for treatment. He refuses and drives her away from the house where he is having such a good time with the city girls. The wife is shocked by her husband's treatment and ungratefulness. She had given him all her money so that he could make a success with his cocoa farm and now he was enjoying his wealth with other women. She sings numerous songs, depicting the ungratefulness of men. Dejected and overwhelmed with grief, she goes to her relatives for treatment.

Not long after her departure, the worker returns to his master, as if destined to be a messenger of bad news, and tells him that his cocoa farm has burned down. The husband is now poor again and has to seek employment. He finds work as an accounts clerk, but he falsifies the accounts and is handed over to the police. Just about the time he is arrested, his blind wife regains her sight and former noble form. She comes to her husband well dressed, only to meet him in handcuffs under police guard. When he is sent to jail, he asks his wife, whom he had denied and sent away, to wait for him and not marry. Despite his maltreatment of her, she still loves him and is sorry for his imprisonment.

Moral: We should not be ungrateful to people who help us. If we are, we suffer for it.

SYNOPSIS 6
TITLE: Think Twice
ORIGINAL LANGUAGE: Twi
PRODUCTION: Golden Stars Band

A man and his nephew, both cocoa farmers living in a remote village called Tumsuosim in the forest area, come to town carrying cocoa on their shoulders to sell. They look drab and dusty and are quite ignorant of town ways. They happen to meet a "boy about town" who claims to know everything that goes on in the town. On seeing the farmer and his nephew, he asks them where they are from and where they are going. They look a bit frightened, but the boy, having discovered that they have money, makes friends with them. He asks the older man, who has lost his wife, whether he wants to get married again. The old man says he needs a wife, and the city boy undertakes to find him one. He takes money from the man. Suspicious of town life, the nephew leaves town to work on the farm while his uncle enjoys himself. The agreement between the farmer and the city boy was that he would pay the boy after he secured a wife for the farmer.

The boy arranges with a certain woman to dupe the farmer and drain him of his accumulated money. Before this happens, the boy collects money from the farmer and provides him with clothes so that he looks like an educated person. He also teaches the farmer a few words in English, including the remark, "that's all." The woman is then introduced to the farmer as a potential wife. She speaks to him in English, and after he has made a mess of the few words he knows, she nevertheless consents to marry him. Because of her coaxing, the farmer gives all his money to the woman, who now bolts. The boy then demands his fee because he had done his part, but the farmer has nothing left to give him. In lieu of pay, the boy takes the farmer's clothes and leaves him only with his pants.

Two nieces come to town and find their uncle in this miserable condition. One of the nieces goes to Tumsuosim to fetch her brother, and they return to town. The nephew tells his uncle that from the proceeds of their farm he has saved £4,000 at the Ghana Commercial Bank, and he puts the money at the uncle's disposal.

He gives the uncle a rich *kente* cloth, which he too is wearing. Before returning to the village, the uncle thanks his nephew for all that he had done and regrets that he had stayed behind to enjoy town life, since it had landed him in misery.

Moral: Men should think twice before they make important decisions. Rash decisions lead to pitiable circumstances.

SYNOPSIS 7
TITLE: Don't Kill Yourself Because of Poverty
ORIGINAL TITLE: Ehia wo a enwu
ORIGINAL LANGUAGE: Twi
PRODUCTION: F. Mica's Band

A certain old man having educated his daughter Agnes (Agi for short) up to university level wants her to marry a palm wine tapper. She refuses to condescend so low, and instead she marries Bob Agoji, a classmate she met during university days. She warns her man from the beginning not to land her in difficulties by deserting her or going out with other women.

Not long after their marriage, Bob Agoji goes away on business and Agi's sisters and a friend from Takoradi arrive for a visit. They try to persuade her to lead a *"jantra"* life (the life of a call girl) which, according to them, is more lucrative than marriage. She could earn money for lots of clothes and shoes and everything else a woman might desire. They sing a song in praise of *"jantra"* life and do everything they can to persuade her to accompany them back to Takoradi. Agi refuses and sings songs denouncing such a way of life. Bob Agoji returns from his trip and finds the *"jantra"* girls in the house. Within a short time he becomes infatuated with them, but nonetheless they depart.

Not long after, a taxi driver comes bearing the sad message that Agi's uncle is dead. Agi leaves to attend the funeral. No sooner has she gone than the Takoradi women come back to Mr. Bob's house. They ask for Agi and learn that she has gone away to attend her uncle's funeral. Wishing to oust Agi from Mr. Bob's affections, the women begin to prejudice his mind by telling lies against her. They say that the taxi driver is Agi's lover and that they have been going out from time to time. They say that Agi has no uncle and that the story of his death was concocted to give Agi and the taxi driver a chance to get away. Mr. Bob becomes so prejudiced

The "college grad," here in drag, has emerged as a popular comic figure in concert parties.

against Agi that when she returns from the funeral, he decides to send her away. No amount of explanation from her satisfies him. When Agi is gone, Mr. Bob then marries one of the *"jantra"* women. Mr. Bob gives her plenty of money, including an amount to give to his new wife's mother, who comes to thank her son-in-law.

Bob Agoji leaves his new wife to go to work, and when he arrives at his office, he finds he has been dismissed. He returns home to tell his wife the unfortunate news. The wife goes to her mother and brings back some money for them to live on, and the mother-in-law also visits him to console him, giving him some more money. A friend of Mr. Bob's visits him and gives him thirty pesewas, and Bob uses twenty-five of them to buy a Ghana National Lottery ticket. When his wife hears of this, she becomes annoyed with him for doing that in their present situation. She goes to tell her mother and they agree she should get a divorce. The mother-in-law comes to Bob's house and insults him for his foolish behavior and she takes her daughter away, thus ending the marriage.

With the help of a Muslim priest who gives him some magic powder, one of Bob's friends is able to persuade Agi's father to let his daughter remarry Bob. Agi comes bringing food to her former husband who is now starving because he is penniless. Accepting it, Bob kneels down and asks Agi to forgive him. She wholeheartedly does.

Not long after Agi's return, it is announced over the radio that Mr. Bob Agoji has won first prize in the national lottery. Thus, within a short period of time, Bob becomes rich and happy again. He has got back his lucky wife, and the lottery ticket that had been the cause of the divorce of his dishonest second wife brings him riches. When she and her mother hear of Bob's new fortunes, they come back to apologize, hoping to obtain some of his money. Bob patiently listens to their pleadings, but he cannot be fooled twice. With the help of Agi's father, Bob drives the *"jantra"* woman and her mother away.

Moral: Man should not try to take his life, as Bob tried when he was starving himself to death, because "where there is life, there is hope." The fortunes of the poor can change at any moment.

SYNOPSIS 8
TITLE: Kwame Ataapim and His Daughters
ORIGINAL LANGUAGE: Fante
PRODUCTION: Bob Cole's Band

Kwame Ataapim, a timber contractor and chairman of the Timber Contractors Association, sends his two daughters to the United Kingdom for further studies. Some time later, his brother dies, leaving a daughter named Awuraa Ekua in his care. Kwame treats Awuraa Ekua very badly. She has no good clothes and in fact owns only one dirty cloth. Not long after, the two daughters, Awuraa Esi and Naana, having studied law and midwifery respectively, return to Ghana. Their father is very happy to see them and gives them a warm, fatherly reception. But upon their arrival, he intensifies his ill-treatment of the orphan niece, and the two daughters also begin to maltreat their cousin. While he refuses to give the niece even a pesewa, he puts all his money at the disposal of his own daughters and spoils them with luxury. The daughters turn their cousin into a maidservant, once even drenching her with water because, they say, she brought it in a dirty glass. Awuraa Ekua weeps and sings, bemoaning her fate.

When Kwasi Twuii, with whom Kwame had been farming for some time, visits him, the two "London ladies" begin to tease and ridicule their father's friend because of his dirty clothes. Poor and in need of money, Kwasi had come to ask Kwame for a loan of £8. He is refused outright, and no amount of entreaty on Kwasi's part works.

Kwasi then tells Kwame that he knows of a fetish priest in Koromantin who can help him with any problem. Kwame replies that because he has refused to give Kwasi any money that he will bring the priest to his house. The priest, called Mframa ("Wind"), comes in full attire, accompanied by an interpreter clad in white cloth. He dances to beautiful traditional drumming, and Kwasi joins in. As is traditional, the priest foretells what will happen to Kwame if he continues to maltreat his niece. This worsens the situation, however, for Awuraa Ekua, and Kwame behaves even more unkindly to her. Fortunately or unfortunately for Kwame, a Mr. Johnson, who had been looking for a job in Accra but without success and who had spent his last cedi on a Ghana National Lottery ticket, arrives to ask Kwame for work. Before agreeing to employ him, Kwame makes his two daughters test Mr. Johnson's English to see if he is as well educated as he claims to be. When Mr. Johnson passes the test, Kwame then decides that he should marry off his unwanted niece to Mr. Johnson, saying that they are equally dirty in appearance.

Because of ill-treatment and poverty, Awuraa Ekua is boorish and rustic. She and her husband find it difficult to live in peace. During this critical period in their life, fortune turns the wheels for them. Mr. Johnson wins £5,000 from the lottery. At the very time he learns this wonderful news, Kwasi Twuii – who had been acting as a sort of unwilling godfather to the couple but had offered them good advice – arrives on the scene, and they all rejoice. Mr. Johnson and Awuraa Ekua then leave for Accra so they can buy themselves new clothes. Returning well-dressed and with plenty of money, they give Kwasi ten cedis to buy clothes for himself.

As fortune would have it, it was at this time that Kwame Ataapim discovers that all the money he had in the bank had been squandered by his daughters. Reduced to poverty, he goes to Kwasi to ask for a loan and is refused. Things go from bad to worse, and shortly thereafter Kwame hears that his daughters have been beaten and wounded at the "Monte Carlo," a nightclub in Cape Coast, and they had been taken to hospital. Soon the daughters come to Kwame's house, wrapped in bandages all over their bodies. Now Kwasi Twuii behaves to them as they had behaved to Awuraa Ekua when she was poor and alone. He throws water in their faces, and beats them and their father too. He asks them whether they – the "London ladies" – would go farm with him at Korforidua. Trembling, the daughters agree. Mr. and Mrs. Johnson refuse to see them before they leave, and marching out under the threat of a cane, the "London ladies" depart for a new life.

Moral: People should not maltreat the children of others, nor pamper their own children. By pampering children, parents make it difficult for their offspring to meet life's challenges.

Notes and References

Chapter 1

1. The following paragraphs on the history of the concert parties draw on the author's own researches conducted over many years. Also consulted are Efua Sutherland, *The Original Bob: The Story of Bob Johnson, Ghana's Ace Comedian* (Accra: Anowuo Educational Publications, 1970); and E. J. Collins, "Comic opera in Ghana," *African Arts,* 9.2 (1976), 50–57.
2. Collins, "Comic opera," 50.
3. Sutherland (*The Original Bob,* 6) notes that tickets cost five shillings, or even ten shillings, a large sum in the 1920s when Yalley was at the peak of his popularity with Ghana's elite.
4. For a brief account of the development of popular music in Ghana, see E. J. Collins, "Ghanaian highlife," *African Arts,* 10.1 (1976), 67–8.
5. Johnson reached Standard Seven at the age of twenty-six in 1930: Sutherland, *The Original Bob,* 6.
6. *Ibid.,* 7.
7. Collins, "Comic opera," 52.
8. Collins, "Ghanaian highlife," 62.
9. Collins, "Comic opera," 50; Sutherland, *The Original Bob,* 8.
10. Sutherland, *The Original Bob,* 12.
11. Collins, "Comic opera," 52.
12. See, for example, *The Two Bobs'* songs in Fante in Sutherland, *The Original Bob,* 10, 11, 14.
13. Collins, "Comic opera," 52; Dennis Austin, *Politics in Ghana, 1946–60* (London: Oxford University Press), 127 n. 41.
14. Collins, "Comic opera," 52.

Chapter 2

1. See the appendix of specimen play synopses: Synopsis 2. Readers may want to read these synopses before they read Chapters 6 to 9.

Chapter 4

1. *The Legon Observer* is the organ of the Legon Society on National Affairs, an independent organization consisting mainly of university teachers and intellectuals.

Chapter 6

1. E. N. Goody, "Fostering of Children in Ghana: a preliminary report," *Ghana Journal of Sociology,* 2 (1966), 26–33.
2. K. A. Busia, *Social Survey of Sekondi-Takoradi* (London: Crown Agents for the Colonies, 1950), 91.
3. Goody, *op. cit.*
4. Ioné Acquah, *Accra Survey* (London: University of London Press, 1958; reprinted Accra: Ghana Universities Press, 1972), 75.

5. Busia, *op. cit.*, 37.
6. *Ibid.*
7. *Ibid.*, 42.

Chapter 9

1. A. R. Radcliffe-Brown, *Structure and Function of Primitive Society* (London: Cohen and West, 1951), 180.
2. R. T. Lapiere and P. A. Farnsworth, *Social Psychology* (New York: MacGraw-Hill, 1959), 396.
3. *Ibid.*, 67.
4. See Robert K. Merton, *Social Theory and Social Structure* (New York: The Free Press, 1957), 19–48.

PART II
Transcripts of Two Concert Parties

Note on the Transcripts of Two Concert Parties

The two concert parties transcribed and translated here were taken down during live performances in Ghana. Both plays bring out the essence of all concert parties in that they deal with common social problems and realities. In particular, the plays discuss the difficulties of married life, the ploys of men (good and evil), and problems relating to in-laws. Although they are comic plays and are presented first and foremost as vehicles to amuse audiences, there is in both an all-pervading religious and moral tone, underlining the fact that Ghanaians are a highly moralistic people.

The synopses of the plays are, briefly, as follows: In *The Jealous Rival,* Araba, a co-wife, realizes that because her rival, Esi, has had a child by their shared husband, Mr. Akwaa, she may have lost her husband's affection and becomes jealous of her co-wife. She approaches Kramo, a Muslim, for help in preparing a charm which is then dropped into the soup prepared by Esi to give to Mr. Akwaa to eat. But her plot is uncovered, and Mr. Akwaa divorces Araba. In *The Ungrateful Husband,* an unattached young woman named Awura Akua meets and marries a bachelor, Yaw Ntow, who, like herself, is given to "good times." When Awura Akua is obliged to visit relatives, her new husband dallies with "ladies" from Takoradi. Awura Akua is hurt badly in an accident, and when the houseboy comes to inform Yaw Ntow of the mishap, he refuses to recognize Awura Akua as his wife. Nonetheless, Awura Akua comes to see him and is disowned. Awura Akua recovers her health and she realizes that her marriage was contracted on false premises. The play concludes on a sadder but wiser note.

Concert parties are live presentations, and in fact there are no set scripts. Rather, the actors work around an agreed-upon plot, leaving much room for improvisation. Musical interludes often appear and are used to suggest a lapse in time in the plot. In transcribing these plays, the author wishes to acknowledge his indebtedness to Miss Patience Addo, who copied the script as it materialized, and to the actors of the companies of the concert parties, who provided the lines.

101

THE JEALOUS RIVAL

Cast

AKWAA: The husband

ARABA: Mr. Akwaa's first wife and "the jealous rival"

ESI: Mr. Akwaa's second wife

FELICIA ⎫
ABENA ⎬ Friends of Araba

KRAMO: A Muslim and maker of charms

KAYA: Head porter and a Hausa

Setting: The play begins with the band playing a highlife number in a loud, jaunty popular rhythm. The scene opens with ARABA, AKWAA *and* ESI *on stage.* ESI *is holding her baby boy.*

Series of highlifes

This life. This life. This life.

This life. This life. This life.

This life is like a mirror, hold it firmly.

This life is like a mirror, hold it firmly.

If you don't hold this life firmly, it will fall down and get broken.

If you don't take good care of this life, it will fall down and get broken.

Don't blame God for being ill-fated in that event.

If you don't take good care of this life, it will fall down and get broken.

Don't blame God for being ill-fated in that event.

This life is like a mirror, hold it firmly.

This life is like a mirror, hold it firmly.

AKWAA   Well, ladies and gentlemen, I have come to this town to work. It is necessary for me to have wives to help me in my work. This is because a man should not work all by himself. When men and women cooperate in work, they achieve

103

greater success in everything they do. This elderly woman (*introducing* ARABA) is Araba. Yes! The young woman (*introducing* ESI) is called Madam Esi. I live with both of them in this town. We have come to this town to work, earn money and take it to our home town. We have come to earn something to take home that is why we are here – Well, just as I have said, the struggle for life is somewhat tough these days, and a man needs to do a lot of calculating, and so life has not been all that enjoyable. Since her (*pointing to* ESI) child is slightly unwell, she needs to go back to our home town for a while. She is going to be treated by the old ladies at home; she will return when the boy recovers his health. I am seeing her off. Now she is going to visit her mother for a while.

ESI   My lord, Kwaku (*smoothing the child's forehead*) has been running a temperature for several days.

AKWAA   Is that right? Well, just a moment. Eh! Are you referring to our child, Araba? All right! There seems to be a mistake somewhere. My name is Akwaa. Yes. . . I am Mr. Akwaa (*to the woman*). What are you telling me?

ESI   I say, Kwaku has been running a temperature these days. I don't know what is wrong with him.

AKWAA   All right! All right! He longs to see his grandmother. Please take him back home. Yes! – He only wishes to see the folks at home. Not until his grandmother has coddled him will his health improve.

ESI   Thank you, my lord, I shall do as you say.

AKWAA   Yes, please do; send him home.

ESI   All right! (*Turning to* ARABA) Sister Araba!

ARABA   Yes; Esi!

ESI   Take good care of the house. God be with you. Goodbye.

ARABA   All right! I shall take good care of the house.

AKWAA   Oh, yes! Wait, wait a minute – have something. (*He takes something from his pocket*) Take this twenty cedis with you to use while you are away.

ESI   (*Turning to* ARABA)   Please thank him on my behalf.

ARABA   All right, I shall do so for you.

ESI   Goodbye for now!

ARABA   Goodbye.

AKWAA   Bye-bye! When you go – (*He whispers something into her ear*) Eh – Araba, are you there?

ARABA   My Lord, I am here.

AKWAA   Yes, as we are wrestling with life's problems, persevere! Do you understand?

ARABA   Eh –

AKWAA   As a woman, when I ask you to sleep, then you sleep, when I ask you to wake up, then you wake. You should obey my word. Do you understand?

ARABA   All right, my lord, it's a long time since we got married and you know my character.

AKWAA   Oh, yes, of course I know.

ARABA   Brethren (*addressing the audience*), I believe that no childless marriage succeeds in this world. A woman has not been successfully married if she bears no children.

AKWAA   Things will be all right, do you understand?

ARABA   (*Again addressing the audience*)   It's quite a long time now since I was married to this man.

AKWAA   Oh yes, yes, we are still together.

ARABA   I have helped him as much as it is humanly possible to help a man.

AKWAA   Things will be all right.

ARABA   It's lack of childbirth which deprives me of social respect. But it's only within the power of God to give children.

AKWAA   Yes, indeed! He will certainly give us children.

ARABA   (*Singing*)   Oh! My stomach –

AKWAA   (*Joining in*)
        I didn't get a childbearing stomach!
        I am pitiable,
        This stomach of mine,
        Has made me wretched among my fellow women.
        This stomach of mine,
        This stomach of mine,

105

Oh, I didn't get a childbearing stomach!
I am pitiable,
This stomach of mine,
This stomach of mine,
Has made me wretched among my fellow women.
This stomach of mine,
The day I shall get a fertile stomach to bear a child,
The day I shall get a fertile stomach to bear a child,
I shall be very happy.
I shall make him my brother and darling,
I shall make him my friend and darling.

ARABA   Eh! My lord.

AKWAA   Eh! Yes, I am listening to you.

ARABA   There is nothing left now, I presume?

AKWAA   Yes, just as I have said.

ARABA   But I am down-hearted.

AKWAA   Yes.

ARABA   However, it's God who gives children.

AKWAA   Yes, I know that.

ARABA   If you agree then —

AKWAA   Excuse me, I should go to work. As we enjoy ourselves we should at the same time be thinking about work.

ARABA   Are you going to work?

AKWAA   Yes, I am going to see about one or two things — Good-bye! *(He leaves)*

ARABA   All right. *(To herself)* Oh! look at a man walking so grace-fully! *(She sings)*
    I love my darling's style of walking
    I love my darling's eyes
    I love my darling's features
    I am dying for my darling
    A slender and stylish young man.
    (She repeats this several times)

AKWAA   *(Returning)*   Well, I nearly forgot! Is everything O.K. in the house?

ARABA   Hmmm!

AKWAA   Goodbye!

ARABA   All right.

AKWAA   Bye-bye! *(He leaves again)*

ARABA *(Soliloquizing)*   Oh God! When shall I have a baby of my own? From now on, I am sure my rival will be more respected and loved by our man. It doesn't matter. Well, I suppose it cannot be helped! My father once told me that the world is full of bitter experiences, but I never believed him. I rather thought the world was a paradise. I now know that the world is full of sorrow. *(She sings)*

> I thought the world was a happy place,
> But the world seems to be a sad place.
> In time of need the whole world becomes a miserable place to live in, even to one's own mother's child one doesn't count for anything.
> Oh, fellow, I am indeed pitiable.
> Even my own friends don't have respect for me now.

(Two women enter as ARABA *sings and wait for a while. Then they begin to speak to her)*

FELICIA   Eih! Sister Araba.

ARABA   Hallo! How are you?

ABENA   Good morning!

FELICIA   What's wrong? Why have you been singing this sorrowful song?

ABENA   I don't understand this sorrowful song.

ARABA   Welcome! *(She shakes hands with them and addresses the audience)* Brethren, these two ladies are intimate friends of mine.

FELICIA   We are on our way to the market this morning, and I thought we should call here to greet you.

ARABA   All right.

FELICIA   The sorrowful song casts a chill over me.

ARABA   I am pitiable!

ABENA   Are you the only pitiable person living?

FELICIA   What is it that has made you so pitiable?

ARABA *[Introducing the two women to the audience]* This friend of mine is called Auntie Felicia and this other one is called Auntie Abena. They are the only friends I have. We began life together. *[Addressing the two friends]* You can see for yourselves what a pitiable life I am leading.

FELICIA Do you think you will remain in this state of life forever?

ARABA You don't seem to have heard what has happened.

FELICIA What is it?

ARABA Since I was married I have done everything! I hoped in vain to get a child. My man has another wife who had a child soon after she was married.

FELICIA Is that so?

ARABA My husband loves the child so much that he does not any time for me at all.

FELICIA Is that what you have been enduring?

ARABA That husband of mine! I don't know what to say.

FELICIA Is that the cause of your singing and what has made you so thin?

ARABA Well, what can I do?

FELICIA Oh! But how does one climb a ladder? Does one jump on it?

ARABA Eih! I don't understand?

FELICIA You climb a ladder step by step, gradually. It is God who bestows childbirth.

ARABA That's true. Very true.

FELICIA Is it childbirth which has been worrying you so much? Look at how lean you have grown!

ARABA Yes! How nice it would be for me to have a baby and put it on my lap.

FELICIA What's nice about that? After all, childrearing is rather a dirty job!

ARABA I gather you have had a baby, haven't you?

FELICIA My husband and I were married for fifteen years before we had a child. I mean fifteen years! For how long have you been married?

ARABA   I have been married for six years now.

FELICIA   Just for six years and you have been worrying so much? Ha! *(She laughs)*

ARABA   *(Joining in the laughter)*   Are you laughing at me? *(They both laugh)*

FELICIA   By the grace of God I had a child after fifteen years.

ARABA   Is that right?

FELICIA   Yes, and you are just pining for a child after having been married for six years.

ARABA   Well, you did well.

FELICIA   Look! Don't behave in the way you are doing.

ARABA   All right.

FELICIA   Eih! You are married, aren't you? Marriage isn't all that easy. *(The three women sing)*
　　Marriage isn't something to trifle with:/:
　　Yet some people seem to trifle with it.
　　It is just left somehow:/:
　　Marriage isn't something to trifle with at all.
　　Marriage isn't something to trifle with at all.
　　Whoever trifles with it harms himself.
　　Yet some people seem to trifle with it.
　　Marriage isn't something to trifle with –
　　It isn't a trifle.

ARABA   *(Addressing the audience)*   Well, brethren, I think I should follow the advice of these friends of mine and stay. No matter what he does to me –

FELICIA   *(Consoling ARABA)*   Never mind! Marriage demands patience, yes, patience!

ARABA   I shall just keep quiet and stay.

FELICIA   You leave everything to God. He will help you.

ARABA   He always gives her *(referring to ESI)* money before he leaves for work.

FELICIA   That's what happens and you should have known that by now. Whatever the condition is, you just keep cool.

ARABA   I accept your advice.

FELICIA   Well, I think we should leave. I am on my way to the market.

ABENA   Is that so? You keep on thinking about a man. I don't think about a man. Well, if you wish to go to the market you may go.

FELICIA   Oh! I came here in company with you, that's why I am reminding you about the market . . .

ABENA   You may go, I shall go later.

ARABA   I presume you are going to prepare meals, aren't you?

FELICIA   Yes, I am going to cook. That's why I am asking her to go with me for company and *(addressing* ABENA*)* do you mean you are staying here until I return?

ARABA   I think it's just because it's a long time since she saw me. Go! She will go later.

ABENA   Mind you, if you don't go and prepare meals and your husband returns, he will certainly beat you. You keep on wasting time. I don't have any man.

ARABA   Aren't you married? Aren't you married as yet?

FELICIA   This girl? Abena! *(Addressing her)* Well, Abena, you may stay with our friend for a while. I should like to go now.

ABENA   All right. Don't be long.

FELICIA   Please keep her company for me. Advise her to rid her mind completely of the worry about childbirth.

ABENA   All right, I'll do so.

FELICIA   Goodbye for now!

ARABA   O.K.

FELICIA   Eih! Abena.

ARABA   All right, goodbye!

FELICIA   I am going; goodbye! I am going and I hope you will find time to come to us to have a chat.

ARABA   All right, goodbye!

FELICIA   I shall be back some time.

ARABA and ABENA   All right.

FELICIA   Don't forget to wait for me here.

ABENA   Oh! I shall certainly wait for you.

(Felicia exits)

ARABA *(Addressing* ABENA)   Are you still unmarried after all these years?

ABENA   You mean marriage?

ARABA   Yes, I mean marriage.

ABENA   Oh, I have got a boyfriend. What's this? Why are you having so much trouble with your marriage?

ARABA   You can't imagine how much suffering I am enduring!

ABENA   Then I presume it won't succeed. *(She pauses)* Look! My new boyfriend holds an enviable post. He has been transferred to Nigeria. In fact, I had to prove my worth to him from the onset when I met him, otherwise he would not have made much of me. But as soon as I started to do it, then—

ARABA   What did you do? Tell me, tell me, tell me what you did. I like to know; I like to know it.

ABENA   It was because of the presence of Felicia, that was why I didn't tell you. Being a lady, she might have commented on it unfavorably if I had told you—

ARABA   What's it?

ABENA   Look!

ARABA   Yes, I am listening.

ABENA   It's something about my new boyfriend.

ARABA   Go on!

ABENA   He didn't make much of me at the beginning.

ARABA   Yes.

ABENA   I happened to consult a certain Muslim who has powerful charms.

ARABA   Is that true?

ABENA   Can you imagine what the Muslim did for me? And now my man—

ARABA   You mean the Muslim did it?

ABENA   Yes. As soon as my man is paid at end of the month, he brings all his money to me.

ARABA   Wonderful!

ABENA   I keep his accounts for him. As soon as he receives his pay, he brings it to me.

ARABA   Oh no! I can't believe that! I can't believe it.

ABENA   I am telling you —

ARABA   My man is very stingy.

ABENA   Oh! You mean you are wondering how to make him become liberal or generous? Well, I don't know what my Muslim is doing right now. I just met him, on my way . . .

ARABA   You mean he has come to this town?

ABENA   Yes, I met him in the market. I even know his house. So if you have any plans —

ARABA   Do you think it is a good thing for me to do? Won't he know what I am doing?

ABENA   Oh! It isn't any elaborate thing which may lead to — It's just a charm which you mix with his food for him to eat and then —

ARABA   It might be a good idea to mix it with palm-nut soup which my man likes so much.

ABENA   Well, if you are inclined to do something —

ARABA   *(Addressing the audience)*   Ah! Brethren, I am sure you will agree with me that what my friend is advising me to do isn't easy to do. I am inclined to believe that —

ABENA   Oh! No! This is something between the two of us. It is a private conversation between the two of us.

ARABA   So I shouldn't tell anybody, eh?

ABENA   No!

ARABA   All right.

ABENA   This is a matter for us alone.

ARABA   I understand.

ABENA   Look, when you come along he *(referring to the Muslim)* will tell you something and then you abide by what he tells you.

ARABA   All right.

ABENA   You will see for yourself what will happen.

ARABA   All right, all right. When is he coming here?

ABENA   If you need him right now, I shall go and call him. I know his house.

ARABA   I am afraid of such things.

ABENA   Oh, what are you afraid of?

ARABA   All right, go and call him.

ABENA   Keep cool; I am going to call him for you and you will see for yourself what he can do for you.

ARABA   All right, I understand, I even don't know how I can thank you adequately. What I really want done is —

ABENA   O.K., I am going to call him here.

ARABA   I am concerned about my rival, my rival, the mere fact that I have a rival —

ABENA   Oh!

ARABA   — he will have to leave her for me —

ABENA   Why worry about that now? *(Preparing to leave)* I shan't keep long.

ARABA   All right.

(ABENA leaves, but doesn't leave the stage. ARABA addresses the audience)

Brethren, my friend has put this idea into my head. Well, I shall think about it.

(KRAMO enters and joins ABENA who accompanies him to ARABA)

ABENA *(Introducing him to ARABA)*   Sister Araba, this is the Muslim about whom I told you.

ARABA   Oh, is this the man?

ABENO   Yes.

KRAMO   Is this your friend who —

ABENA   Yes.

KRAMO   Well, Madam.

ARABA   Yes.

KRAMO   *[Addressing* ABENA*]*   Is this the woman who sent for me?

ABENA   Yes, that is my friend about whom I talked to you.

ARABA   Well, she herself suggested that she was going to call you for me.

*[*KRAMO *plays with his beads and talismans]*

KRAMO   There is something to tell you. *[He turns toward* ARABA *and begins to divine]*

ARABA   I thought as much; you fellows always have something to tell people.

KRAMO   There is certainly something to tell you. You are a good woman, but you are unable to produce children.

ARABA   Ah!

KRAMO   You are childless.

ARABA   Eih, this is wonderful! This is a wonderful man.

KRAMO   Your husband has another woman, a woman . . . She is a stout woman . . .

ARABA   Yes.

KRAMO   You are a very pitiable person; your mother is poor and your father is also poor.

ARABA   My lord, what have I done?

KRAMO   I pity you a great deal.

ARABA   Ao!

KRAMO   Had it not been for this lady *[he turns toward* ABENA*]*, I wouldn't have come here.

ARABA   No, you wouldn't have come here.

KRAMO   Madam.

ARABA   Yes.

KRAMO   You are—

ARABA   What?

KRAMO   You are a beautiful woman; but your husband dislikes you when he sees you. No matter what you put on, whether it be a cloth, a scarf, a pair of shoes, he simply doesn't like you. He doesn't even like you for cooking, for preparing stew, fufu or rice. Whatever you do he simply doesn't like you. Now, I tell you one thing; you aren't a person who would kill another person. You have never killed a person.

ARABA   No.

KRAMO   I shall give you something.

ARABA   All right.

KRAMO   You will put it into your husband's food.

ARABA   You mean into his food?

KRAMO   Yes.

ARABA   Is it good to put this charm into palm-nut soup?

KRAMO   You can put into any food or soup.

ARABA   I asked this question because my husband likes palm-nut soup very much.

KRAMO   You will cook pork.

ARABA   Pork! My husband doesn't like it.

KRAMO   Well, you will cook pork.

ARABA   I am afraid. He has never eaten pork.

KRAMO   You will mix the charm and the pork for him, and don't you partake of the food. You shouldn't have any of that food at all. It's only your husband and that fair-colored woman who should eat it –

ARABA   Shouldn't I even taste it?

KRAMO   No! Not at all!

ARABA   All right.

KRAMO   It's only your husband and the other woman who should eat it.

ARABA   I see!

KRAMO   After eating that food –

ARABA   Yes –

KRAMO   Your husband will cease liking that fair-colored woman; he will completely dislike her. You will then realize how powerful I am.

115

ARABA   All right, I agree. By the way, how much will you charge me for this?

KRAMO   I really pity your present condition.

ARABA   All right.

KRAMO   I shan't charge you anything. I just want it to be finished, first.

ARABA   All right.

KRAMO   I shall accept whatever you have for me in the end.

ARABA   O.K. I understand. Thanks a lot. Eh! Abena? *(She turns to* ABENA*)*

KRAMO   This is really a very good woman – I beg to leave now.

ARABA   All right, keep fit. It remains one thing, can I add a crab to the soup?

KRAMO   Oh yes! It doesn't matter.

ARABA   All right.

KRAMO   Well, I must leave now. *(*KRAMO *exits)*

ARABA   Well, you have really made me happy now. I hope by the grace of God if everything works as planned, my husband will henceforth love me very well.

ABENA   He even mentioned a particular point, namely that you are under the charm of your kinsfolk –

ARABA   Look! That man is wonderful. He divined my problem just like that.

ABENA   He has divined that a grandmother of yours has been the cause of your childlessness. Nobody knows what she gains from it.

ARABA   Well, now by the grace of God, things will be all right. By the grace of God, things will be well with me.

(Musical interlude begins)

ABENA *(Advising* ARABA*)*   Sister Araba, enjoy yourself.

ARABA   At the moment I don't think I should worry about anything; by the grace of God –

(Singing)
You think I shall never prosper; by the grace of God, I have prospered!

It hurts you, Oh! brother:/:
You thought I wouldn't prosper.
By the grace of Almighty God, I have prospered now.
Brother, it hurts you! It hurts you!

[The two women sing and dance]

ARABA   Eh! eh! You know what? eh? I had wanted to tell you. I shan't let my husband see this stuff at all. I am going to prepare food and put it into the food.

ABENA   Well, if you handle it well, the result will be good for you.

ARABA   I shall do so.

ABENA   But if you don't handle it well—

ARABA   You say what? So long as he eats palm-nut soup, I shall prepare it for him. Thank you so much. Why not sit down?

ABENA   Oh, I should like to be permitted to go home now.

ARABA   You mean it?

ABENA   I'd rather you no longer worry about your rival.

ARABA   All right.

ABENA   Good!

ARABA   I shall simply rid my mind of any thoughts about her and just prepare the charm.

ABENA   Well, if you don't do that you will have yourself to blame. So do your best to—

ARABA   All right.

ABENA   As soon as he comes.

ARABA   All right.

ABENA   You make it a point to humor him and do whatever he wants done for him.

ARABA   I'll do that.

ABENA   Have patience to do what you have in mind to do.

ARABA   All right, I'll do so—don't forget to visit me again.

ABENA   All right—goodbye for now.

ARABA   Bye-bye!

ABENA   Try by all means to do it.

ARABA   I shall try to do it by all means.

(ABENA leaves and there is another musical interlude)

ARABA *(Soliloquizing)*   I see! Is that what my kinsfolk are doing to me wherever I go for divination I am told I am under the sorcery of my kinsfolk? *(She sings)*

> Go ahead and kill me, my kinsfolk!
> Do kill me in time,
> Kill me, for I love to die —
> Please waste no time, kill me,
> Kill me, I truly love to die.
> I am motherless,
> So do kill me quickly,
> Kill me, I love to die.

(Returning from work, AKWAA enters)

ARABA   Hallo! Are you back?

AKWAA   How is everything in the house?

ARABA   Everything is all right.

AKWAA   Where is my food?

ARABA   I beg your pardon!

AKWAA   I am asking about my food.

ARABA *(Hesitating)*   Your food, I haven't prepared it yet.

AKWAA   What? You mean you haven't prepared my food, what do you expect me to eat?

ARABA   Oh! Are you annoyed, dear? Have patience please.

AKWAA   I am going out to find out something. I shall be back soon. You understand?

ARABA   Yes, I understand.

AKWAA   I hope by the time I return, everything will be ready. Do you understand?

ARABA   Yes, I do.

AKWAA   All right, I won't be long. Don't forget my likes?

ARABA   What likes?

AKWAA   You mean after all these years you haven't learned my favorite soup?

ARABA   What is it?

AKWAA *(Shouting)*   Don't you feel how cold it is and you still ask me what it is? Palm-nut soup!

ARABA   Palm-nut soup, indeed. Did you give me any money when you were leaving? With what did you think I should buy food to cook?

(AKWAA gives her some money and goes out)

ARABA *(Thinking aloud)*   Shall I prepare palm-nut soup? *(She pauses a long while)* No, I shan't prepare any palm-nut soup. Well, I know what I want to do, my plans are set on the sort of thing I want to do –

(AKWAA returns)

AKWAA   Did I leave a book behind? I seem to forget official things.

ARABA   Did you leave anything with me?

AKWAA   Well, I am just looking for it.

ARABA   What are you looking for?

AKWAA   Do you mean you have finished spending all the money I gave you to buy food to cook? I am surprised. If you are not prepared to cook the food, why take the money? Do you want it for your own food? You better emulate your rival.

ARABA   What are you saying?

AKWAA   Well, I am going to send her a telegram right now.

ARABA   To whom do you say you are going to send a telegram?

AKWAA   I am going to send a telegram asking her to come back.

ARABA   Go ahead, send her a telegram. I have no doubts at all that that wife of yours is – Send a telegram asking her to come.

AKWAA   Look, if you don't take care, I'll let her come. No doubt you know her well. She does her cooking from a book.

ARABA   Mind you, my Lord, the old order changes. Please note that.

AKWAA   The old order changes, eh? I will write to her to come.

ARABA   I have done a lot for you and this is my reward. *(She sings)*

119

I have toiled in vain without commendation
Let somebody else take her turn :/:
Just because I am childless nobody makes much of me.
I am my mother's only child.
I am miserable in this world.

(Time lapses. Enter KAYA *and* ESI, *carrying her baby)*

KAYA Hei! Madam, could you help me to put my load down?

ESI Hallo! Sister Araba!

KAYA Hei! Madam, could you help me to put down my load?

ARABA Oh! Come on, get out of my way!

KAYA Won't you help me to put my load down?

ARABA Why don't you ask the other person standing there to help you?

ESI *(To* ARABA) What harm will it do you if you help him, Sister Araba?

ARABA *(Replying)* Shame! Get out of my way!

KAYA *(Addressing* ARABA) Hei, Madam, don't be silly!

*(*ARABA *and* KAYA *exchange insults while* ESI *tries to stop them.* AKWAA *enters)*

AKWAA What's wrong?

KAYA This woman *(waving angrily at* ARABA) refused to help me put my load down when I arrived here.

*(*ARABA *and* KAYA *resume the quarrel)*

AKWAA Where are the police? *(He looks searchingly out of the window for a policeman)*

ESI Please, Mr. Akwaa, pay the porter and let him go. I haven't paid him.

KAYA This woman *(looking toward* ARABA) is silly. She is not a good woman. If she doesn't take care I will beat her right now.

AKWAA *(To* ARABA) I think these people *(nodding in the direction of* KAYA) are always difficult.

KAYA This fair-colored woman *(gesturing to* ESI) is a good woman. You *(gesturing to* ARABA) are not a good woman.

AKWAA *(Protesting to the porter)* Now, stop that! Take your money and go away.

KAYA *(Singing to tease* ARABA*)*   Your head is as big as that of a soldier. Ei!

AKWAA   Kaya, cut that out!

KAYA   She is not a good woman. Look at her head like . . .

AKWAA   Kaya, please stop that!

KAYA   Silly woman. Bloody fool!

*(*ARABA *rushes towards* KAYA*)*

AKWAA *(Speaking to* ARABA *and then to* KAYA*)*   Look! Take care you don't find yourself thrashed by him! Kaya, stop that and go! *(*KAYA *exits.* AKWAA *turns to* ARABA*)* Look! Take this from me. If you ever pick a quarrel with anybody like that again, I shall leave you to it. Do you think —

ARABA   Do you expect me to keep mute while he insults me? Should I allow myself to be insulted in that way?

AKWAA   You refuse to cook and to make use of the money given you for that purpose. And you have just picked a quarrel with a head porter. *(He turns to speak to* ESI*)* Esi, please prepare something for me to eat. I am so annoyed that I feel like going out and having some beer to cool my temper.

AKWAA *(Speaking to* ARABA*)*   Look, you saw the stick which the head porter was holding. It is an evil stick! You won't live a year when he hits you with it. *(Turning to* ESI*)* Hallo! Darling, I shall be back soon.

ESI   All right.

AKWAA   Try your best to find something — because I am hard up now —

ARABA   Yes, I thought as much. That's what's the matter now.

AKWAA   What is?

ARABA   That's what's the matter now.

AKWAA   What is? *(Turning to* ESI*)* I am going out and shall be back soon.

ESI   All right.

AKWAA   You know yourself that I won't be long.

ESI   O.K.

AKWAA *(Cuddling the baby)*   Daa! daa! daa! daa!

ARABA   That's enough!

AKWAA   Look, this is my own child...Don't give the child anything.

ARABA *(Singing)*

> I have submitted myself to this kind of treatment –
> Treat me in any way you like.
> Brethren, let them treat me in any way they desire;
> Everything has a cause.
> I have submitted myself to it.
> My enemies may treat me in any way they like.
> I have submitted myself to it.
> You may treat me in any way you like.

ESI   Sister Araba, I hope you will take care of the food I am putting on the fire? I am going to buy salt. I shan't be long.

ARABA   All right, you may go.

ESI   I shall return very soon.

ARABA   All right. I shan't leave this place. I shall take care of it for you. Go and buy the salt.

> *(ESI exits)*

ARABA *(Speaking to the baby)*   Don't look at me. *(She drops the charm into the food on the fire. A little later* ESI *returns, lifts the lid of the pan on the fire and shows that she notices a change)*

ESI   Sister Araba, what has changed the color of this food?

ARABA   Have you seen me touching the food?

ESI   Eh! I fear you, Araba. Araba, you seem to be a witch.

ARABA   You, rather, are a witch. You are a witch.

ESI   Araba, I fear you; I really fear you.

ARABA   You, rather, are a witch. You are a witch.

ESI   What did you put into the food, Araba?

ARABA   I haven't put anything into it. I just tried to put things right when I noticed that the food wasn't cooking well.

ESI   But what has happened to the food? What is the matter with it? You, witch; Araba, I fear you.

ARABA   You are the person to be feared. You are to be feared. Get out of my way!

122

ESI   Shame! I fear you. You are to be feared. Just because I have had a child you are stung by jealousy.

(AKWAA enters)

AKWAA   What's the matter? What's wrong?

ESI   You want to know? Araba has committed a murderous act in this house. Look, look, look at this potion.

AKWAA   What is it?

ESI   Look, look in front of you. I can't touch it.

AKWAA   What is it? *(He goes to see the potion)*

ESI   I had better collect my child and go away. Just because I have a child, there is a plan to kill me and my child.

AKWAA   Now tell me what it is?

ESI   Look at the potion lying there. I can't go near it.

AKWAA   *(Looking and shouting at ARABA)*   Shame!! By jove! What is it? Hei! Come here, come here.

ARABA   What do you want me for? I am not coming!

AKWAA   By jove! I didn't know you had such a potion with you in this house. I see. *(He claps his hands)*

ESI   I swear, I can't continue with a marriage of this kind. If I do, my mother will only hear of my death. Araba, you are a wicked woman; you want to kill me –

ARABA   You are a wicked woman; you are a witch.

ESI   Araba, I quit, you can have the marriage to yourself. Because of the child I have had as a result of this marriage, you want to kill me and the child. I quit! I can't carry on with the marriage any longer. *(She turns to AKWAA)* Keep her as your only wife. I don't want to be killed.

AKWAA   Look! Wait, wait. I am going to tell my people about it.

ESI   No! I can't agree to that.

AKWAA   No, I won't. Eh! Araba, I didn't know you were a person to be feared.

AKWAA and ESI   *(Expressing surprise)*   Eh! Araba!

ESI   Well, I am going.

AKWAA   Please, please don't go.

ESI   Kaya! Kaya! *(She calls for* KAYA *to help carry her things away)* Where has this porter gone?

AKWAA   I even don't know whether this potion is gunpowder or what.

ESI   Hei! hei! Kaya!

KAYA *(Entering)*   Any load for me to carry? Any load for me?

ESI   Kaya, please take these things and let us go. I am leaving my husband.

AKWAA   Has this man *(pointing to* KAYA*)* come back again?

ESI   You know what? This woman has put something into my food.

KAYA   Well, I told you. I told you that this woman is not good.

ARABA   Oh, get out of here! *(She throws something at him)* Get out!

KAYA   This woman is not a good woman. If you continue *(addressing* AKWAA*)* to have this woman as your wife, you will die and your other wife will also die. *(He attempts to hit* ARABA *with his stick, but* ESI *and* AKWAA *intercept)*

AKWAA   Well, if he had hit you with the stick and killed you, that would have ended everything.

ARABA   I would have hit him back with a stick.

KAYA   You are bound to die soon. Shame on you! Madam Esi, you keep cool.

AKWAA   I shall come over to see your father.

ESI   Well, I don't think your visit to my father will help in this case.

AKWAA   It's my child. And I am much more concerned about him. My child –

ESI *(Speaking to* ARABA*)*   This is your husband. I have left him for you alone.

AKWAA   Oh, look –

ESI   Just because of the child I had in this marriage there is a plan to kill me and my child. I quit, I shan't stay as his wife any longer. There is your husband for you alone. Shame! Shame on you. Witch! A devil incarnate! *(She and* KAYA *start to go)*

AKWAA Are you really going away? Oh, don't be so annoyed.

KAYA This woman— *(KAYA and ARABA look menacingly at each other; then ESI and KAYA leave the stage)*

AKWAA Araba, I hope you knew what you were in for. It was lucky I held him, otherwise he would have hit you on the head with a stick, and that would have been your death. Why did you behave in such a way? Were you counting on any help? Now, tell me, what are you up to? You don't do any cooking in this house. But when another woman is cooking, you have gone out of your way to meddle with her food just because you have long arms.

ARABA The point is, my lord, the point is. . .

AKWAA Yes, tell me what made you go for a charm to kill me.

ARABA The point is—

AKWAA Let us know whom you wanted to kill—

ARABA The point is you were once quite different to me.

AKWAA If I was once different, you were different too.

ARABA I mean our relationship in the past was different, it was better, I think you realize that? When you married a second wife, I realized that you loved her better than me. And then when my friend came here she gave me—

AKWAA Ha! ha! ha! You mean I love her more than you?

ARABA That wasn't a charm to kill you or my rival. It was rather a charm to make us all cooperate and live in harmony.

AKWAA Now make your point clear. You mean you want the three of us to cooperate or you want the two of us—you and I to cooperate?

ARABA My only wish is that, eh! You know, I thought you loved her more than you loved me, that was why—

AKWAA And so you have decided to put a charm into my soup so that I would change my mind about you? Oh, what a strange world. So that is the purpose of what you have done, eh? You are to be feared!

ARABA Please, I hope you will understand, I didn't intend to kill you with the charm.

AKWAA   But I am afraid of something which when I have swallowed it will change my mind. I fear you because of that.

ARABA   Please forgive me; I shan't do it again.

AKWAA   You are asking for forgiveness. This is what you did while your rival was here – I am sure with her absent you will do worse things. You will give me more charms to swallow. Yes, I am sure of it.

ARABA   Well, as I said, it isn't a charm to kill you or my rival, it is just something for –

AKWAA   Is it your own charm?

ARABA   A friend brought it –

AKWAA   A friend? She has ruined you. By the way, do you know the plans which your friend has in mind?

ARABA   Please forgive me.

AKWAA   It's all right for you to ask me to forgive you. But I am sure my spirit will not forgive you. I am going to tell your father about it. I am going to tell him that you have been putting charms into my soup.

ARABA   My God! Are you divorcing me?

AKWAA   It isn't I who am divorcing you; what you have done leaves me in no doubt that you want to go away yourself. I am just going to find your father so that he can come and see what you have been doing.

ARABA   *(Singing)*

> If I have offended you in any way, please forgive me.
> In whatever way I have offended you,
> Please forgive me.
> (She repeats the song)

AKWAA   *(Addressing the audience)*   Ladies and gentlemen, do you agree with what she is saying? I am sure if a gunman aimed his gun at any of you, you wouldn't wait for him to shoot you, would you? *(To* ARABA*)* Well, you have said what you have in your mind, I am also thinking about my life. I am going to ask your father to come for you. I hope you won't indulge in charms when you go to your father. I shan't be long.

ARABA   Please, pardon me. It's a friend who has landed me in these difficulties. It isn't my fault.

126

AKWAA   I shall be deceiving you if I promise that I shall continue to live with you as my wife.

ARABA   Oh, please! You have known my character ever since we were married.

AKWAA   But you now obtain charms to harm me. *(He exits)*

ARABA   Oh, God! I now realize that by this evil deed I have ruined my marriage. *(She sings)*

> Brethren, truth no longer exists, truth no longer exists,
> My people, truth no longer exists. Let us be on our guard –
> Be wary of whatever you do together with another person,
> If you don't you will only find that he has betrayed you.
> Don't divulge your secrets to anybody.
> Man is a treacherous being,
> He may pretend to love you, but the next moment you will find him undermining you.
> Look, I have found myself in these terrible predicaments because of the machinations of a person intimate to me.

(AKWAA returns from a visit to ARABA's father)

AKWAA   Well, I was told your father had gone to Accra. I shall go to Accra myself by whatever means people go there. Whether they go by train or by lorry, I am going there by the same means.

ARABA   Please, my lord, pardon me. For God's sake, forgive me.

AKWAA   Now, you haven't had a child by our marriage, and by your conduct you have driven away the woman who has had a child by me. You think I am going to waste my time on you? *(He exits)*

ARABA   Oh! This situation would not have arisen if my friend had not encouraged me to do it. *(She sings)*

> Truth no longer exists...
> *(She repeats the song she has just sung)*

(Speaking moralizingly to the audience) Brethren, I am now convinced that in this world of ours, if you are born a woman and you get married to a man you must try by your conduct to prove a worthy wife to your husband. Obey him, and don't try to influence him by means of charms; avoid making many friends.

It's no insult if your husband tells you not to make many friends. You should know when your husband is hungry and provide him with food. If you do all these things, then your marriage will be a success. At the moment, I don't know what to say when I go back to my people. I shall recount my adventure when I arrive home. *(She sings)*

O, poor traveler,
Everyone travels in search of wealth.
If I have struggled in vain,
I put my trust in You,
God, I put my trust in You.

I shall recount my problems to my people the day I arrive home.
I shall recount the numerous problems and incidents encountered in my adventure.
O God, I have trust in You.
When I arrive home, I shall recount my problems to my people.

It is threatening to rain.
Look at the skies!
The stars are twinkling!
O God, I rely on You,
When I arrive home.

(Addressing the audience) Well, brethren, I am going. My piece of advice to the women among you is that they should let this example serve as a warning to them. They should try to be of good character when married. *(She sings)*

Brethren, life is a struggle:/:
Don't envy somebody's acquired wealth:/:
Brethren, life is a struggle:/:

THE END

THE UNGRATEFUL HUSBAND

Cast

AWURA AKUA (AKUA): A motherless young woman who wants to be married

MAN/FATHER YAW NTOW: A young man from Akuapem who marries her

OLD MAN/KWASI AYIPE: Awura Akua's father and a farmer with traditional ways

BROTHER/JOE SMART: Awura Akua's brother

GYIMA: Yaw Ntow's servant who befriends Awura Akua and stays with her

DONKO
(MADAM) YAA ASANTEWAA } "Good-time girls" from Takoradi

Setting: A simple and bare stage, a platform with a group of bandsmen seated at the left side. There are two microphones on the stage, one for the bandsmen and the other, in the center of the stage, for the actors. After the introduction of the group, the band plays a series of highlifes. The actor (or actress) playing the part of AWURA AKUA *comes on stage and addresses the audience.*

AKUA *(Addressing the audience)* Honorable countrymen, ladies and gentlemen, lads and lassies now gathered here, my story is that I am a lady who had traveled far and wide in this world without any gains. I have therefore come back home. There is no place like home. I have reached a marriageable age and I should like to get married. I am therefore inviting any young man who is also of a marriageable age to come, for I am available for marriage. *(She sings)*

> A poor wanderer:/:
> A poor wanderer,
> I am looking for an unmarried man to marry me.
> *(She repeats)*

AKUA Well, gentlemen, I am aware that it is embarrassing to do certain things in public. Whoever has an interest in me can come home. If he does come everything will be made easy for him. Goodbye! *(She starts to leave but sees a man of about her own age dressed in dirty and shabby clothes)*

AKUA   Oh, my! Look, young man, come here. Young man, come!

MAN   O.K. I am coming.

AKUA   What is it? Are you afraid of me?

MAN   No, I am not afraid of you.

AKUA   Aren't you a man?

MAN   I am a man. I am coming.

AKUA   But why are you shuddering so much?

MAN   *(Nervously)*   Oh, I am not shuddering! I am just standing here.

AKUA   Do you say you are over there?

MAN   Yes.

AKUA   Yes, I am listening to you.

MAN   Hmm! I was on my way to the college to collect something of mine from a friend when I heard somebody singing and I decided to come and see the singer.

AKUA   Right, and can you sing?

MAN   You mean sing a song?

AKUA   Yes.

MAN   Well, I sing a little.

AKUA   Then listen to me. *(She sings)*

A poor wanderer:/:
A poor wanderer
I am looking for an unmarried man to marry.

MAN   *(Singing)*

A poor wanderer:/:
A poor wanderer
I am looking for an unmarried woman to . . . hmm.

AKUA   Hallo, young man! Hallo, young man!

MAN   Yes, lady.

AKUA   Oh, I am very happy.

MAN   *(Laughing)*   Ha! ha!

AKUA   You really are a very good singer.

MAN   Is that so?

AKUA   Pardon me, what's your name?

MAN   My name?

AKUA   Yes.

MAN   I am called Father Yaw Ntow.

AKUA   Father Yaw Ntow?

NTOW   Yes.

AKUA   Where do you come from? Are you an Akuapem?

NTOW   Yes, I am an Akuapem.

AKUA   But how come that you speak Fanti so well?

NTOW   Well, as regards the Fanti language, I had my schooling at Cape Coast and that's when I learnt it.

AKUA   I really don't believe that you are an Akuapem. If you really are an Akuapem, then take your time and speak a little bit of Akuapem in my hearing.

NTOW   Look, lady, do you think if I weren't an Akuapem, I could deliberately deceive you by telling you that I was an Akuapem?

AKUA   Well, pardon me, Father Yaw Ntow, I am so delighted you are a very good singer. I fell for you as soon as I saw you.

NTOW   Is that right?

AKUA   I love you more than my mother. I am not bothered by the clothes you are wearing. It's your person in which I am interested.

NTOW   All right.

AKUA   Look, are you listening? I am offering you myself as a "scholarship."* Do you understand?

---

*"Scholarship" here is a term used figuratively to describe a situation when a woman offers herself freely to a man as a lover and cares for him "all expenses paid," instead of the normal practice of the man asking for her love and caring for her.

NTOW   Is that right?

AKUA   What do you need? Money? I will give you more than enough. I will buy as many suits as you want for yourself. Do you need a car? You shall have it.

NTOW   Do you really mean a car?

AKUA   I shall buy one for you.

NTOW   You mean you can afford to buy a car for me?

AKUA   That's nothing!

NTOW   But who told you that I have a driving license?

AKUA   Well pardon me, Father Yaw Ntow –

NTOW   All right.

AKUA   I have some reservations about getting married during a visit. However, my name is Awura Akua.

NTOW   Awura Akua.

AKUA   And my father's name is Kwasi Ayipe.

NTOW   Kwasi Ayipe!

AKUA   As regards my mother, she is dead.

NTOW   Hm!

AKUA   I am left with my father and brother.

NTOW   All right.

AKUA   Three of us are occupying one house.

NTOW   Just the three of you?

AKUA   I should like to direct you to my father for you to discuss matters with him concerning our marriage and for you to reach a clear understanding with him.

NTOW   In order to reach a clear understanding with him? Hm –

AKUA   Yes, so that in case you travel with me and any mishap such as death occurs, you will be in a position to send my body back home without any blame.

NTOW   Are you prepared to go along with me for better or worse?

AKUA   Oh, yes, I am prepared even to die with you if need be.

NTOW   I too, on my honor, am prepared to remain with you through thick and thin.

AKUA   All right. I think, on the onset, I should ask for your permission to go and discuss matters with my father so that we reach some understanding. That will also enable me to know his feeling about the whole matter. And I shall let you know it, so that when you later go with me to see my family, everything will be easy for you.

NTOW   All right, that's reasonable. You may go.

AKUA   Well, take care of yourself and the house until I come back.

NTOW   All right, I shan't leave the house for any place; you will come and meet me in the house.

(AKUA *exits. Then she returns and sings)*

AKUA   *(Singing)*

You are the one I love.
You are the one I love, my darling.
(She repeats this refrain several times)

(AKUA *continues)*

Oh! Father Yaw Ntow!

NTOW   Lady.

AKUA   Oh, I am happy. You are an expert dancer.

NTOW   You haven't seen much of my dancing yet. By the way, what happened when you spoke to your father?

AKUA   Well, I have discussed everything with my father and he is thrilled about it, because he thinks I am of age, and if I plan to get married, it's good. However, he would like to meet the young man. He would like to meet you. He would like to meet his son-in-law, so that if the son-in-law happens to travel with me then he will know what sort of man I am with. I am sure you understand?

NTOW   Oh, yes, I do.

AKUA   Mr. Ntow. I should now like you to go to my home and see my people.

NTOW   I shall do so.

AKUA   What did I tell you is my father's name?

NTOW   He is called e –

AKUA   Father Kwasi Ayipe.

NTOW   Father Kwasi Ayipe.

AKUA   Keep on reciting it to yourself – "Father Kwasi Ayipe" so
that you don't forget it.

NTOW   I shan't forget it.

AKUA   Well, then, that's all.

NTOW   All right, that's all! *(He sings)*

> Married people have gone to bed after meals,
> And I, a bachelor, am wandering about aimlessly.
> They have gone to bed after meals,
> And I am wandering about aimlessly.

AKUA   *(Joining in the singing)*

> Married people have gone to bed after meals
> And I, an unmarried person, am wandering through the
> streets aimlessly.
> Oh, poverty is a miserable state to be in.
> They have gone to bed after meals,
> And I, an unmarried person, am wandering about aimlessly.
> Married people have gone to bed after meals,
> And I, an unmarried person, am wandering about aimlessly.

(Enter OLD MAN, dressed in traditional attire)

AKUA   You are welcome, father.

OLD MAN   Thank you, Awura Akua, thank you, thank you.

AKUA   Well, Pa, would you like to tell us the purpose of your visit?

OLD MAN   You came to tell me that you have met a certain young
man here with whom you have fallen in love.

AKUA   Yes.

OLD MAN   And I told you to ask him to come and see me.

AKUA   That's so.

OLD MAN   But no sooner had you left than a car arrived from
Accra with a message that all senior farmers were wanted in
Accra.

AKUA   Is that right?

OLD MAN   Yes, we are to meet in the Farmer's Hall.

AKUA   Is that so?

OLD MAN   And you know I am the farmers' leader so it is necessary for me to arrive there before the meeting begins.

AKUA   That's right.

OLD MAN   I have just called to tell you that I am on my way to attend the meeting, but after the meeting, I shall return so that you can ask the young man to come and see me. That's what I have come to tell you.

AKUA   All right, Pa, I am pleased with what you are telling me. However, the young man is here right now and I should like you to speak to him so that when you return from the meeting, you will have had time to consider whatever he says. Don't you agree?

OLD MAN   I am afraid there isn't time for that. I have to go to the meeting at once.

AKUA   Father, I know you have to, but he is in this house now so just let me call him.

OLD MAN   Oh, no, I don't want to waste any more time.

AKUA   I know that.

OLD MAN   You know yourself that I should be there before the meeting begins.

AKUA   That's true.

OLD MAN   Look here! You know yourself what time it is now and you insist on waiting. Why look at the time! I am needed most urgently.

AKUA   You are right.

   (The OLD MAN *looks at the time from a huge table clock tied with a lady's silk handkerchief round his left wrist. It was previously hidden in his cloth)*

AKUA   Oh, Pa!

OLD MAN   I am supposed to be there before the meeting opens. And it is about time I got there. Look at the time yourself! It's six o'clock. Why should I waste any more time?

AKUA   Oh, but what you are wearing is a table clock and not a wrist watch!

135

OLD MAN   Is it a table clock?

AKUA   Yes, it is, we have one even there.

OLD MAN   Oh, you are a child, just a child. You have no idea
about it. Look, I presume you bought this small watch *(he points
at* AKUA*'s wrist watch)* for six pounds. This big one I am wearing
costs only twenty-five shillings. Which of these two watches do
you think is better? When I wear this big one, nobody keeps
asking me what time it is because as soon as anybody sees it
from afar, he immediately knows what time it is and so there is
no need for him to ask me. Thus I save myself the trouble of
having to answer people's questions about time just because I
have bought a watch. This is certainly an improvement on your
small watch.

AKUA   You are quite right. As an older person what you are
saying is right. Pardon me, Pa, I like to remind you of what I
told you earlier. I should like you to meet the young man now,
so that by the time you return from the meeting you will have
had a chance to consider the matter. Please oblige me.

OLD MAN   Oh, all this is a waste of time! Now look, if the young
man is here, as you say, then call him.

AKUA   Well, Pa, he is the one standing right by you.

OLD MAN   Eh! Do you mean to tell me that of the many young
men in this town you haven't met any whom you can love but
this one?

AKUA   Yes, Pa. He is the only one I love. "One man's meat is another man's poison," so goes the proverb. I love him as he is.

OLD MAN   Are you telling me "One man's meat is another man's
poison?"

AKUA   Yes.

OLD MAN   So is this your poison? Ha! ha! ha! *(laughing)* Awura
Akua, you are not a choosey lady at all. *(He continues to laugh)*
And so...God Almighty...Awura Akua, you have truly
brought something into this house! *(He jeers at* NTOW *and continues to laugh)* Now tell me which part of a man like this at-
tracts you—is it his face or the back of his head? *(He continues to
laugh and holds his ribs)* Oh my ribs, my chest!

AKUA   Pa, it was you who told me to go and look for the man I wanted to marry. If I have met the man I love, it is for you to give me your blessings. We shall be married according to our native custom. Father, are you going to sanction this marriage?

OLD MAN Just because I have asked you to look for the man you like, you have to fall for this? *(Laughing)* Well, it's all right, perhaps I have old eyes and that's why I don't see him clearly, ha! ha! ha! I don't think I can raise any objection now. "Each for himself and God for us all!" "One man's meat is another man's poison!" Therefore, if you have decided that this is the man you love, then I can't say anything against your choice. But what's your name, young man? What's your name?

NTOW *(Stammering and shivering)* I am...am...am...

OLD MAN Ha! ha! ha! hii! hii! But Awura Akua, what's wrong with your man? Is he shivery or does he suffer from fits?

AKUA Ha! Pa, he's a young man who stammers a lot. He stammers a lot before he is able to speak. It takes him hours before he is able to speak.

OLD MAN What? Then you have made a wrong choice! *(He pauses thoughtfully)* Does he stammer so much?

AKUA Yes.

OLD MAN But don't stammerers just stammer with their mouths? And this... *(he laughs)*. Look young man, what's your name?

AKUA Please, Pa, he is called Father Yaw Ntow.

OLD MAN Father Yaw Ntow.

AKUA That is it.

OLD MAN The name seems to fit him very well – Yaw Ntow! Hmm – that's why he is shaking in this way. *(He laughs and looks at* YAW NTOW*)* What work do you do?

NTOW Nsawam.*

OLD MAN Nsawam! Eh, what's the matter? Is he deaf? When I am asking him about his work he gives me the name of a town – Nsawam. Is Nsawam a profession or an occupation?

AKUA Pa, he didn't hear you. I am nearer to you but I didn't hear you well. He thought you asked for his place of work.

---

*Nsawam is a town 24 miles north of Accra.

OLD MAN   I see, it means he works at Nsawam, hmmm. I should
think the jobs in Nsawam are very easy to do. Ha! ha! ha! – I too
should go and try my hands at the jobs in Nsawam. Ha! ha!
ha! Well, and good! Awura Akua, what work does he do?

> *(NTOW tries to answer but, as a stammerer, he has difficulty in
> doing so; he stamps his foot on the stage and demonstrates the
> work he does with his hands, indicating how he maneuvers a
> steering wheel of a truck)*

NTOW   I . . . I . . . I . . .

OLD MAN   *(Laughing and asking NTOW)*   Don't you hear? What are
you trying to demonstrate? Are you a boxer or what?

AKUA   He is a driver. A driver. A driver.

OLD MAN   A driver of what?

AKUA   A taxi driver.

OLD MAN   A taxi driver! Don't you think if taxi drivers drove the
way he has demonstrated they would break their arms? Eh! If
this is the way a taxi is driven, then I wonder how a caterpillar
truck would be driven. Awura Akua – It's really good!

AKUA   Father?

OLD MAN   I can't witness this alone. Go and call your elder
brother to come and see his brother-in-law – *(laughing)* – Yaw
Ntow!

> *(AKUA exits and returns with her BROTHER. In the meantime
> the OLD MAN and NTOW out-stare each other)*

BROTHER   Old Man, here I am.

OLD MAN   Are you here? Well, if you are, we have something to
tell you.

BROTHER   What is it?

OLD MAN   Hm! This is what we have to tell you. Hasn't your sister
told you about it?

BROTHER   About what, Old Man?

OLD MAN   This is what has happened.

BROTHER   What is it? She hasn't told me anything.

OLD MAN   Do you mean to tell me that Awura Akua didn't tell you
anything when she came to call you?

(AKUA has been scratching BROTHER's head)

BROTHER *(Addressing AKUA)* What's the matter, why have you been scratching me?

OLD MAN What's the matter?

BROTHER She has been scratching me since we left to come here and she continues to do so now, in public.

OLD MAN Why is she scratching you? *(Addressing AWURA AKUA)* You, why have you been scratching his head?

AKUA Pa, I am just playing with him. Don't I have a right to scratch my own brother?

OLD MAN Eh! This means that those of you *(making a sign to the audience)* who have sisters should be careful when you are moving about with them, or else by scratching you they may cause rashes on your bodies. *(Addressing his son)* Well, the facts of the case are this. She says she has met a man whom she loves; she even dotes upon him. She finds it difficult to eat when he is absent. But I find it difficult to realize that this is the man. And so I decided to invite you here to see your brother-in-law with your own eyes.

BROTHER Now where is that brother-in-law of mine?

OLD MAN You mean your brother-in-law, hmmm! He is sitting right beside me. He is sitting here.

BROTHER How are you, brother-in-law?

NTOW I...I...I am fine!

BROTHER Old Man, I have seen my brother-in-law; I approve of the marriage. It's in order.

OLD MAN What are you telling me? Is something wrong with your eyes? Such a man is asking for your sister's hand and you rashly say, "I approve of the marriage"?

BROTHER He is all right. My reason for approving is this. If he is the wrong type, as soon as he sees a woman whom he plans to marry, he will make all sorts of promises to the woman. He will tell her, I shall give you this and that. If he doesn't have clothes he will borrow very beautiful ones from a friend and wear them to impress the woman. When he wins the woman's love and the owner of the clothes comes to collect them, then he will be left with nothing. Wealth is not acquired in one day. It has a

139

gradual beginning. Old Man, you should approve of the marriage.

[NTOW *is pleased and so he bluffs*]

OLD MAN   Just because his brother-in-law is pleading for him, he *(pointing at* NTOW*)* is swollen-headed and is pretending that he is enjoying life. I don't see what life you are enjoying. *(He laughs)* And you *(addressing his son)*, if somebody happens to see your sister and this young man together and asks you your relationship to the young man, what will you say?

BROTHER   Old man, perhaps one day I may prosper through this so I approve of the match.

OLD MAN   Do you think you will one day prosper through this man? Well, when a poor person promises to give you a hat to wear, the absence of a hat on his head should make you know what to expect from the promise. Do you think you will one day prosper through this man? How prosperous is he to be able to make you prosper? Well, I have nothing to say. You and your sister are the same. If this is the man she wishes to marry, then it is senseless for me to waste my time any longer. I should attend the meeting now. I am attending a meeting and I shall return when it is over and we shall then talk about the marriage. Let the young man be with you here until I return.

AKUA   All right, Pa, don't be long.

BROTHER   All right, goodbye Old Man.

OLD MAN   Right! *(He turns to go)*

BROTHER   Old Man, your son-in-law is calling you.

NTOW   Ha...hav...have this pou...pound for you...your tax...taxi fare.

OLD MAN   What? You want me to have a pound for my taxi fare? Young man, a pound from this dress of yours? *(Deriding* NTOW*'s dress)* Keep it. *(Laughing)* I don't think I can accept a pound from this dress. Keep it. If I do accept money from this dress of yours and put it into my pocket, all the money I have in my house will disappear during the day. I am all right. I have already kept some money for my taxi fare. You know what? I don't make demands on any suitor of my daughter – Awura Akua, you take this for yourself *(giving her money)* in case things don't turn out as expected –

AKUA   All right, Pa *(*BROTHER *tries to join her in receiving the money from their father, and* AKUA *reproves him).* He says Awura Akua —

OLD MAN   What's the matter, won't you allow your elder brother to listen to what I shall tell you? Why do you prevent him from doing so?

*(*AKUA *and her* BROTHER *struggle over the money)*

AKUA   Pa, you were talking to me, weren't you?

OLD MAN   Oh no, stop it. It doesn't become you to behave like that. After all, he is your elder brother. *(*OLD MAN *pauses and then continues)* You shouldn't treat him like that. . . . I am not quite sure how long I shall be gone so the two of you take this money for your use in case you come to need it. I am going and I shall come back. See you again!

AKUA   Oh, Pa, you see what he is doing —

(A few coins fall to the ground and BROTHER *is about to put them in his pocket when* AKUA *draws their father's attention to them)*

AKUA   Pa, some of your coins have dropped. Take them.

OLD MAN   Eh! So smart? Do you wish to pilfer now as you have pilfered in my house? Whenever I am checking my money at home and I leave the money for a while, I return to find that he has pilfered some of it. In fact, his original name was "Yaw Joe" but because of his smartness in snatching money I have re-named him "Joe Smart." *(Addressing* BROTHER*)* You must stop pilfering. Stop it! Don't do it again.

AKUA   Pa, look, he still has some of the money.

OLD MAN   How did you know that he still has some of the money on him?

AKUA   I just know it.

OLD MAN   This is why he often beats you. You have seen him with the money and you insist that he still has some money on him. You know, as soon as I leave he will probably give you a severe thrashing.

AKUA   Pa, I would like to search him. If nothing is found on him after the search he is at liberty to do whatever he likes to me.

OLD MAN   Do you wish to search him?

AKUA   Yes.

OLD MAN   Look, Joe Smart, come here and let her search you. If she doesn't find anything on you, I am here and I shall allow you –

BROTHER   Oh no, Old Man, there is nothing on me. There is nothing on me! *(Feigning a stomach ache)* I have pains in my belly.

> *(AKUA searches his pockets for money)*

OLD MAN   That's the only pocket he has.

AKUA   Please have patience, Pa. Are you the one searching him?

OLD MAN   Eh! Are you turning yourself into a policewoman?

AKUA   Look, Pa. I have seen it. There it is.

BROTHER   Oh, my tummy *(feigning illness because of embarrassment)*, I am suffering from stomach ache.

OLD MAN   Where is it? What is it? Let me see it.

AKUA   Here it is! Look, it's here *(dipping her hand into her BROTHER's pocket)*.

BROTHER   *(Continuing to feign illness)*   I have a stomach ache.

OLD MAN   Now take out your hand from your pocket and let me satisfy myself. Eh, Joe Smart!

> *(Annoyed at the embarrassment she has caused him, her BROTHER attempts to slap her)*

AKUA   Oh! Pa, he is –

OLD MAN   *(Questioning BROTHER)*   What are you doing? Do you intend beating her? There are policemen here. Go ahead and beat her. In the first place, you have stolen some money. That's the first charge against you. You are making matters worse by beating somebody, and that will be the second charge. Do you think that's a good thing? Look, it's high time you stopped pilfering. Never do it again!

BROTHER   *(Pleading sorrowfully)*   Old Man, will you please give me some of the money?

OLD MAN   Do you want me to give you some money? What are you going to do with it?

AKUA   What do you want money for? I am the third child after you and you are still unmarried and getting old. You are fed free. Of what use are you?

OLD MAN   You have heard what your younger sister is telling you, that your marriage is overdue. Therefore, look for a woman so that I can perform the customary rites for the marriage and bear all the expenses. You always get annoyed as soon as I mention this question of your marriage. You hate marriage. *[Addressing the audience]* The other day, I myself looked for a woman, performed all the preliminary rites connected with the marriage, and asked him just to go and see the woman. He bolted away to Accra and stayed there for two months, and I decided to go after him. He hates women, that's why! I don't know why he hates women so much. The slightest talk about women annoys him. *[Addressing* BROTHER *again]* Does it mean you love yourself too much or that you are impotent? I simply can't understand why you don't want to have anything to do with women! I shall take you to the hospital today for you to have a medical examination. Yes, I shall get a doctor to examine you to find what is wrong with you. You know very well that it is because of you that I have been toiling all my life. You are my only son. Very soon I shall be no more. You should marry, have children and name them after me. I have explained everything, without avail. You have made me toil in vain. *[He sings]*

It is for nothing that I have been toiling throughout my life:/:

AKUA and BROTHER   *[Joining in]*

It is for my future life that I have been toiling.
Yes, it is for my future prosperity that I have been toiling so much.

OLD MAN   Hm! Well, I guess I should go now. Yes, I should go. Awura Akua, take good care of the house

AKUA   All right, Pa.

OLD MAN   Hmm! Yes, I should go. I shan't be long.

AKUA   All right, Pa, so long! *[*OLD MAN *steps on his dress]* Pa, take care you don't fall.

OLD MAN   Oh, my dress is disturbing me. Tighten my belt well for me. Goodbye.

AKUA   All right, Pa – goodbye. *[*OLD MAN *exits]*

BROTHER   Awura Akua, come and stand here and – come on here, my brother-in-law. You see that large crowd of people gathered there. They are each well-dressed and groomed. It's you alone who are shabbily dressed. Just look at the dress you yourself are wearing. What sort of impression do you think you make wearing this oversize dress and standing before such a crowd. Why do you do it?

NTOW   Ah! My brother-in-law, I am disheartened by your re-marks. Remember one has got to cut one's coat according to one's cloth.

AKUA, NTOW and BROTHER   *(Singing)*

> O! Brother, your fellow men are moving ahead with the times.
> An orphan, why are you lagging behind in this race for progress?
> O! Brother, your fellow men are moving ahead in life,
> Why are you idling away your time?
> Well, good fellow, "each for himself and God for us all."
> I have tried my hands at almost every work in vain.
> Poverty haunts me. Whatever I do, I don't prosper.
> All this is because I am being bewitched by my kinsmen.

BROTHER   Now, come here, Awura Akua, and you, too, my brother-in-law. Now do you see yourself brother-in-law, a young man wearing this type of dress and walking through the streets of modern Ghana? Akua, I can imagine you using the money which Pa gave you to buy clothes for this young man, only to be deserted by him soon later.

AKUA   Oh, no! My husband won't treat me that way! You better get married yourself and mind your own business. Stop it; stop talking like that. Even if he deserts me that isn't your look-out. Please stop filling my ears with such remarks.

BROTHER   Well, Awura Akua, this is my advice. You know that misfortune can come in anybody's way in this world.

NTOW   Oh, please stop discussing things like that. Everybody doesn't see things as you do.

BROTHER   *(Singing)*

> My sister, stop all this noise:/:
> My sister, stop all this noise:/:

As regards your newly acquired darling,
You must know that trouble haunts every man,
Misfortune haunts every man,
Mishaps haunt every human being.
Such a person should not be brought into the house,
I have warned you;
Pay heed when you are advised,
Or else you will run into trouble.

AKUA and NTOW *(Singing)*

All that you have said has fallen on a deaf ear:/:
Once I have decided to die with him,
Whatever you do, I shall die with him.

BROTHER Awura Akua, if this is the man you have decided to marry, then you better get him new clothes. I should like to say goodbye to you and go.

AKUA I shall provide him with everything he needs.

BROTHER *(Singing)*

Provide him with money when he is in need of it.
Provide him with clothes when he needs them.
Provide him with shoes when he needs them.
If you don't care for him, I may some day have to care for him.
This dear sister of mine will provide for him.
I shall provide him with money when he needs it.
If you don't care for him, I may some day have to care for him.
This dear sister of mine, please, do care for him,
My only beloved darling, do care for him.
Please do provide for him.
If you don't care for him, I may some day have to care for you.
I shall provide him with money when he needs it.
If you don't care for him I may some day have to care for him.

Well, Awura Akua and my brother-in-law, I shall leave now. Please take good care of my sister for me, my brother-in-law. With regard to our father; he is an old man now. He has one foot in the grave – Hm! Well, that's life.

145

NTOW I am grateful to you for what you have done for me. I never expected such amazing kindness from you.

BROTHER Goodbye for now, I am on my way.

NTOW All right. . . . My brother-in-law, are you on your way? *(He softly remarks that he has no money)* I am really amazed at your kindness to me, I can't think of any other person who would show a similar kindness to me. Please take this one pound (NTOW *offers it to him)* for your lorry fare; please take it, you may use it in buying at least cigarettes on your way.

BROTHER All right, Awura Akua, you haven't given me some of the money Pa gave to us and you have disgraced me over it. Thank you so much my brother-in-law.

NTOW Don't mention it. You don't need to thank me. I have only given you what was given to me *(smiling at* AKUA*)*.

AKUA My sisters, women gathered here *(addressing the women in the audience)*, that is what you should all do. If you get married and your husband is poor, help him to work. When he becomes rich he too may some day help you. It is good to help each other. There is an Akan proverb which says "the right hand washes the left hand and the left hand too washes the right hand."

NTOW That's right!

AKUA Darling, you are eloquent now, but were unable to speak when Pa was here. I had to save the situation, otherwise it would have been very embarrassing.

NTOW Eh! Did you think I wasn't eloquent?

AKUA But what happened when my Pa was here?

NTOW I am quite eloquent, but you know when he came I was hard up and I had to behave that way – Are you there, darling, Awura Akua?

AKUA Oh, yes, I am here, darling!

NTOW What I'd like to tell you is this. You have been extremely kind to me. You know? I was once rich. I had a lot of money.

AKUA I am aware of the fact you were once rich.

NTOW As soon as all my money was gone, all my houseboys deserted me.

AKUA That's what happens in life. People flock to a rich man, but as soon as he becomes poor, they desert and disown him.

NTOW   I am now left with one Nigerian boy.

AKUA   Is he living with you?

NTOW   Yes, he is living with me.

AKUA   Didn't he desert you when you became poor?

NTOW   He is with me. He is a good boy.

AKUA   Call him here. After all, he is a fellow human being; please call him here.

NTOW   I will call him here.

AKUA   Poor fellow, probably he is even hungry. Call him here.

NTOW   Well, here he is. This is my houseboy. *(NTOW introduces GYIMA, who comes onstage, to the audience)*

GYIMA   Good evening to you all!

NTOW   He's my boy.

AKUA   Is that so?

NTOW   Yes, he is called Gyima. *(Introducing GYIMA to AWURA AKUA)* Gyima, this is my wife. I told you about her. Her name is Awura Akua.

AKUA   Welcome, Gyima.

GYIMA   Thank you, Auntie.

AKUA   How are you?

GYIMA   I am fine, thank you.

AKUA   How is your mother?

GYIMA   She's all right.

AKUA   How is your whole family?

GYIMA   All my people are in good health. *(Turning to NTOW)* Master, is this your wife?

NTOW   Yes.

AKUA   Well, darling, I'd like to ask for your permission and leave now. I'd like to go home for a few minutes. Why don't the two of you sing and dance happily together. I shan't be long.

GYIMA and NTOW *(Together)*   All right.

AKUA   Goodbye for now!

GYIMA and NTOW   All right, goodbye.

AKUA   Goodbye.

GYIMA   Auntie, please buy something for me when you are coming back.

AKUA   What would you like?

GYIMA   Buy me some sweets, please!

AKUA   All right. *(She exits)*

NTOW   Look *(addressing his houseboy)*, why are you always fond of food wherever you go?

GYIMA   *(Reproachfully)*   Do you think God created our tummies for nothing? They are for food.

NTOW   Let us sing and dance.

> *(They dance, and* GYIMA *sings)*

AKUA   *(Entering)*   Hallo, darling!

NTOW   Ah!

AKUA   I am so happy.

NTOW   All right.

AKUA   I suggest you go home for a short while.

NTOW   All right.

AKUA   But don't keep long. I have something to discuss with you, so go and get yourself cleaned up and come back.

NTOW   All right! All right! I shan't be long.

GYIMA   Master.

NTOW   Stay here with Auntie. You understand? I shall be back soon.

GYIMA   All right. Goodbye.

> *(*NTOW *exits)*

AKUA   Look, Gyima, at the moment your master is not here. You know that?

GYIMA   That's right!

AKUA   Please don't get annoyed. You understand? Have you eaten today?

GYIMA   Food? I haven't eaten anything at all.

AKUA   Why?

GYIMA   There is no money.

AKUA   There is no money? Oh! poor fellow! There is no money. Take this shilling piece to buy some food to eat, you understand?

GYIMA   Thank you so much, Auntie. I shall work well for you tomorrow morning.

AKUA   Well, Gyima, in the absence of your master, I guess we should make ourselves happy by singing and dancing, do you understand? *Gye ani.*

GYIMA   You mean you want to "take one of my eyes" *(misinterpreting what his mistress says).*

AKUA   Oh, no! Why, don't you understand the Twi language? When I say *Gye ani,* I mean we are to make ourselves happy, not the literal translation. What I said means to entertain ourselves, do you understand?

GYIMA   Oh, you mean entertainment? I thought you meant you wanted my eyes!

AKUA   Well, Gyima, what song can you sing?

GYIMA   A song? "Express your love."

AKUA   "Express your love." You mean I should express my love? Express my love to whom?

GYIMA   I should like you to express your love for my master.

AKUA   You are clever. I shall express my love for him. Now begin a song and let us sing.

AKUA and GYIAMA   *(Singing together, with musical accompaniment)*

> Express your love, express your love,
> Express your love for me to see;
> Express your love, express your love,
> Express your love for someone else to to see.

AKUA   *(Laughing)*   Ha! ha! ha!

AKUA   *(Singing)*

> I sometimes feel cold, my darling.
> Come and entertain me.
> Your absence sometimes casts a chill over me.

GYIMA *[Joining in]*

> Come and entertain me.
> My darling, I sometimes don't feel well,
> My love, come and entertain me.
> My dear love, come and entertain me.

AKUA *[Singing longingly]*

> Morning dew is falling,
> Yaw Donko*
> Is falling elsewhere,
> Yaw Donko,
> My darling, Yaw Donko ee! ee!
> My darling is gone,
> Yaw Donko,
> It's long since my darling went away,
> Yaw Donko,
> I long to see him,
> Yaw Donko,
> Darling, I am overwhelmed by loneliness
> Yaw Donko ee! ee!

> *[NTOW enters dressed very well]*

NTOW   Look, Gyima, what have you been doing since I went away?

AKUA   Hello! Darling, have patience!

NTOW   What?

AKUA   I could see your boy likes entertainment, so I asked him to make himself happy.

NTOW   What?

AKUA   There is nothing wrong about what we are doing.

NTOW   No. That's all right!

GYIMA   Well, I am first! *[Declaring himself first in his dancing competition with AKUA]*

NTOW   Are you there, Awura Akua?

AKUA   Yes, I am here.

---

*Yaw Donko is the name used for "Darling" here.

NTOW   I have been away longer than I expected, but there is nothing wrong. It is just that —

AKUA   Eh, I beg your pardon —

NTOW   Is there anything wrong? — Well, I have managed to secure a job and I am to attend work at 6:30 a.m. The man in charge of our section has asked me to bring about four pounds for a —

AKUA   What, four pounds?

NTOW   Yes.

AKUA   You mean he is demanding that?

NTOW   He says I should take it. This demand has set me thinking and I don't know where I can get the money. Why, could you lend me the four pounds, so that if in future you are ever in need of money I will also help you?

AKUA   Well, that's what is expected of a wife. I am so happy that you have secured a job for yourself. It's a very good idea. Can you imagine me not helping you, my husband, to get employment because of this small amount of four pounds? *(Addressing the women in the audience)* Women, make it a point to help your husbands when they are in need of financial help, because the struggle for life isn't easy. *(AKUA hands the four pounds to NTOW)*

AKUA   Darling, is that the correct amount?

NTOW   Yes, it is.

AKUA   All right.

GYIMA   *(Warningly)*   Eh, Auntie, what are you giving him the money for?

AKUA   You don't understand. Your master has got a job and he will be at work by six-thirty in the morning. That's why I am giving him money.

GYIMA   *(Teasingly)*   Is that the reason why you have given him money? Eh! Successful marriage!

AKUA   Darling!

NTOW   Hallo, darling!

AKUA   I would like to have your permission to leave.

NTOW   All right.

AKUA   I am going to spend a few days with my Pa in Accra and shall return in due course.

NTOW   All right.

AKUA   Darling, put energy and enthusiasm into your work.

NTOW   All right.

AKUA   I am going to have some discussions with him about you. I think you understand, don't you?

NTOW   Yes, I do.

AKUA   As I have told you previously, if by the time I come you have started working, then I shall buy a car for you and employ a driver to drive it. I wouldn't like you to be walking to work.

NTOW   All right, all right, I understand.

AKUA   *(Giving money to* GYIMA*)*   Gyima, take this to buy food to eat, I am going to visit my Pa. I shall be back within three days, you understand?

GYIMA   All right, I shall use the money sparingly.

AKUA   Yes, be sparing with it.

GYIMA   All right, thank you.

AKUA   *(Addressing* NTOW*)*   I am of the opinion that if you, a young man, wander about with empty pockets, you won't feel easy. You may meet friends who buy drinks for you and spend around four shillings. As custom demands, you should return their kind gesture by buying them some drinks; if you fail to do so, it will be a disgrace to you, so take this pound as pocket money. You might need some money to buy cigarettes or something.

NTOW   I still have a pound of the two pounds you have already given me —

AKUA   Well, have this in addition, because as a man, it doesn't matter even if you have ten pounds on you, does it?

NTOW   *(Pretending not to want to take the money)*   Oh, it's all right, keep it, keep it, keep it —

AKUA   Oh! No! Take it, take it. Do you want to put me to shame?

NTOW   No, I don't intend to put you to shame.

GYIMA   As for Master, when Auntie is giving you money, you better take it and stop bluffing. *(Addressing* AKUA*)* Hallo! Auntie, please buy something for me when you are returning. Buy fried red plantain for my Master.

*(*AKUA *exits nodding and waving her hand in agreement)*

NTOW   That's right.

GYIMA   Now I shall tell you something.

NTOW   What is it you want to tell me?

GYIMA   When you came and Auntie Awura Akua consented to marry you, you were in shabby clothes, like a head porter; you remember?

NTOW   Yes, I do. I was in tattered clothes.

GYIMA   So you realize that Auntie loves you and that's why she has given you money to spend at your work. She has done this, so that you can earn more money for your family. But you seem to have got it into your head that she has plenty of money and you are encouraged by that idea to do whatever you like, wherever you go.

NTOW   Well, that's quite true. What you are saying is quite true.

(Enter DONKO *and* YAA ASANTEWAA; DONKO *is singing)*

DONKO   *(Singing)*

Edusei resembles the son and not the grandson of a chief:/:
I am in a predicament, but it doesn't behoove a man to shed tears in a predicament:/:
That's me Edusei, look at the predicament in which I am.
Edusei resembles the son and not the grandson of a chief.

(The two women see NTOW*)*

DONKO   Hallo, young man!

*(*NTOW *pretends he doesn't hear)*

DONKO   Now look, young man, won't you answer my call? Good even! Come here!

NTOW *(Reluctantly)*   Thank you.... I am alone, by myself, here —

DONKO   How are you?

GYIMA Eh! What are you doing? What do you want here? What do you want here? Now look, you must know that here it is not a Kumasi hotel, do you understand?

DONKO *(Cheekily)* It's a Nigerian hotel to the Nigerian boy.

GYIMA *(Returning the insult)* I'm your uncle.

DONKO A Nigerian, a snail eater!

GYIMA *(Cheekily but firmly)* It's your grandpa who is a snail eater – My master hasn't time for you today.

DONKO Look, young man *(addressing* NTOW*)*, please tell me what is this fellow *(pointing to* GYIMA*)* doing here?

NTOW He is my own boy. He is sometimes a bit off his head.

DONKO Is that right? You better find time to send him to a mental hospital, an asylum.

NTOW Right, I have myself decided to send him to an asylum tomorrow.

DONKO Please do so.

NTOW Oh, yes, I'll send him there, my dear lady.

DONKO Well, our mission is simple and pleasant. We live in Takoradi,* and we were on our way to Tema when we heard your music; we are music lovers and so we have been naturally compelled to call here.

NTOW Is that so?

DONKO Yes.

NTOW Well, there is nothing amiss here. I am Father Yaw Ntow, a rich man.

GYIMA *(With feeling)* Master, I should say so!

DONKO Really? Are you Father Yaw Ntow, the rich man?

NTOW Have you heard about me?

DONKO Oh, yes, I have heard your name, but I don't know you.

GYIMA Eh!

NTOW Now, what's the name of the other lady who is standing over there?

---

*Takoradi is a city noted in Ghana for "good-time girls."

YAA   You mean me?

NTOW   Yes.

YAA   I am called Madam Yaa Asantewaa.

NTOW   Madam Yaa Asantewaa. How about you? *(speaking to* DONKO*)*

DONKO   My name is Donko.

NTOW   Donko.

DONKO   Yes.

NTOW   Well, the news here is this: I am Father Yaw Ntow, the rich man of this area. It is the elders of this area who have gathered here tonight. The fact is, I shall be leaving for overseas tomorrow, you know? And they have gathered here to give me a send-off party. I am therefore looking for respectable ladies like you to meet me here at five o'clock tomorrow evening so that I may take you with me to overseas.

YAA   *(Showing some doubts about what* NTOW *has said)*   You mean to the U.K.?

NTOW   Look here, you may enquire from all these people here, and let me save my breath.

YAA   Why don't you come over here, Sister Donko?

DONKO   *(Moving to* YAA*)*   Right, here I am.

YAA   This gentleman *(pointing at* NTOW*)* suggests that he would like to take us overseas. What do you think about that?

DONKO   *(Excitedly)*   Eh! I will go! You want to know what I think about it? You know that my mother has never been overseas!

YAA   You are quite right.

DONKO   Even my father hasn't been overseas.

YAA   That's so.

DONKO   If by the grace of God, I, Donko, have been offered a chance to go overseas, should I decline this offer? I certainly shall go.

YAA   There you are! Please come, my lord *(to* NTOW*)*. You see, we are just travelers and if you want to go overseas with us, we are very grateful to you. We shall indeed go with you.

NTOW *(Offering money to* YAA*)*   Take this and use it for the lorry fare to bring your things, your baggage, here.

YAA   No, thanks!

DONKO   Not now.

NTOW   Why not, when will you take it and go?

DONKO   Thank you so much but –

NTOW   You better hurry up, don't waste time at all.

YAA   Well – Father Yaw Ntow.

NTOW   Yes, you better hurry up.

YAA   Pardon me, I would like to ask you one question.

NTOW *(Assuming an air of importance)*   Well, go on.

YAA   Are you sure that you, on your own, can take both of us overseas?

NTOW   Look at what I have here in my hand *(he shows a bundle of paper money to her)*. I haven't even touched my pocket yet.

YAA   Is that right?

NTOW   Yes.

YAA   That's all right, then.

NTOW *(Singing)*

    I say I need you at five o'clock.
    Come when it's five o'clock.
    This is an agreement with my lovers.
    Come along when it's five o'clock.
    Asantewa ee!
    Come when it's five o'clock:/:
    This is an agreement with my lovers,
    Come when it's five o'clock.
    (Pause)
    They will come, come to entertain me,
    My dear will come when it's five o'clock.

YAA *(Singing)*

    I shall come when it's five o'clock.
    Brethren ee!
    I shall come when it's five o'clock.

156

It's agreed between my darling and me that
I shall come when it's five o'clock.

ALL *(Singing)*

We shall come when it's five o'clock
(They repeat as a refrain)

> *(As the women exeunt, the* BROTHER *enters, but he has been
> watching the scene for some time)*

BROTHER *(Addressing* NTOW*)* My brother-in-law! (showing surprise at his behavior with the two ladies)

GYIMA *(Imitating the* BROTHER*)* Eh! Brother-in-law!

BROTHER *(to* NTOW*)* My brother-in-law!

GYIMA *(Getting in their way)* Brother-in-law.

BROTHER Oh, get out of here, get out of here . . . Who is this —

GYIMA Why do you push me around? It is your sister Awura Akua who is married to my master. I am thinking of her!

NTOW He is my houseboy, he is my boy!

GYIMA Hee!

BROTHER Is he your boy?

NTOW Yes.

BROTHER These good-time women are always troublesome. Just in this short interval since my sister left, they have made their way to this place — *(Turning to* NTOW*)* Brother-in-law, where is my sister?

NTOW Oh! I am sorry I haven't yet told you everything. You can see my present condition since I met your sister here. I don't even have words to describe her. Look at this cloth *(indicating the kente cloth)*. She bought it for me. In addition to that, she has given me money to spend at my work. I can't imagine a more generous woman. . . . You have a wealthy family — You really have a wealthy family!

BROTHER Well, you are wearing *kente*. Lucky you! My brother-in-law, I have heard all that you have been telling me because I am as experienced as you are. On my way here I met two ladies at the gate. By the way they were behaving, singing, and mentioning your name in their songs, I immediately realized that they had visited you.

157

NTOW   Do you think they came from this place?

BROTHER   I presume it was because they saw you in an expensive *kente* that they came here.

NTOW   What do you mean? I dislike such remarks. Don't make such remarks to me.

BROTHER   But at the beginning –

NTOW   You can ask all these people whether the ladies have been here.

BROTHER   I can repeat the song they were singing to you.

NTOW   What was the song?

BROTHER   Just listen to it. Brethren, the song was this *(singing):*

> They will come when it's five o'clock,
> Brother-in-law the ladies say,
> They will come when it's five o'clock, they will surely come,
>   to have a pleasant chat with you.
> Brother-in-law, they will come when it's five o'clock.
> Brother-in-law, they will come when it's five o'clock.
> Brother-in-law, your women say that they will come when
>   it's five o'clock to discuss marital affairs with you.
> They say they will come when it's five o'clock.

> *(Continuing)*

Brother-in-law, you may take this from me. With very few exceptions, the ladies of these days are not reliable.

NTOW   Not reliable in what respect? In what respect do you mean?

BROTHER   There are some women who remain ungrateful even when their men have built storeyed buildings for them to live in.

NTOW   In what respect?

BROTHER   Listen! The secret affairs you have with other women aren't at all good. Brother-in-law, women hide a lot from us men, and we hardly realize it. To be frank, you are lucky in the wife you have chosen. I am sure you realize that. See, Akua has even bought a fine *kente* cloth for you, while I, the brother, don't have any! You better take great care of her because she is good.

NTOW   Please, stop making such remarks. I am not in any way an
ungrateful person.

BROTHER *[Singing]*

>   Modern women aren't good!
>   Pardon my bluntness —
>   Modern women aren't good, they aren't at all good, they
>   aren't good!
>   They aren't honest to men.
>   Modern women aren't at all good.
>   Ladies and gentlemen,
>   Modern women aren't at all good.
>   Ladies and gentlemen,
>   A certain woman had an only daughter,
>   The daughter's boyfriend was Kwadwo,
>   Her husband was Kwasi,
>   And Kofi, too, was her boyfriend:/:
>   How many men does this woman have?
>   Kofi too was one of the men.
>   The woman happened to be pregnant,
>   Ladies and gentlemen, now gathered here,
>   The woman became pregnant and as she lay in her room,
>   She began to think very seriously about the whole thing.
>   The question was, was she to tell Kwado that she was ex-
>   pecting a baby?
>   Or was she to tell Kwasi?
>   Or was she to tell Kofi?
>   Thus the matter kept her thinking, and complaining!

>   *[Continuing after a pause]*

>   It set her thinking,
>   As well as complaining.
>   When the time for the childbirth was due,
>   She could not give birth to the child because of her sins; and
>   so she died in labor.
>   When the lady's mother was mourning her daughter,
>   Ladies and gentlemen, she stated in her wailing that it was
>   witches who had killed her daughter —
>   But it was her daughter's misdeeds which resulted in her
>   death.
>   It was her unstable sexual life which caused her death:/:

> Modern women aren't good!
> Brother-in-law, these modern women aren't good, they aren't good!
> Modern women are not at all good!

GYIMA   They have dubious and cross-grained ways.

NTOW   What do you imply by this? Tell me, what's the meaning of all this?

BROTHER   *(Singing)*

> What people enjoy saying to a man is,
> "Condolences, poor fellow!"
> What people always wish to say to a man is,
> "Condolences, poor fellow!"
> Brother-in-law, you were really poor, in dire need of even threepence –
> "Condolences, poor fellow!"
> You lacked even a decent common cloth, brother-in-law –
> "Condolences, poor fellow!"
> My sister had to buy you a cloth and you are now making love to other women –
> "Condolences, poor fellow!"
> Brother-in-law, be careful or else you will have regrets –
> "Condolences, poor fellow!"

> *(Continuing)*

I have nothing more to say to you. I am going away.

NTOW   Go away! Let me think quietly about my problems.

BROTHER   All right, I am going. *(He sings)*

> The days of kindness in this world seem to have passed.
> Brethren, all sorts of things happen in the world these days.
> When one does a kindness these days, one receives evil in return.
> Remember what kindness has once been done to you and show your love to us.

> *(Continuing after a pause)*

If you still wish to go after those women, go ahead. When your cup of happiness is full, it will surely spill over. I have nothing more to say about it. If you continue with those women, I can assure you, in less than two weeks you will be poor again. Then you will realize your folly!

160

NTOW I don't want to hear such remarks! *(He sings)*

It doesn't pay to act in accordance with the wishes of modern women.
Brother-in-law, it doesn't pay to conform to their wishes,
If you do, you have to buy them a pair of shoes, you will have to buy them cloth
Hm! Baby, baby pancake!
You will become penniless.

BROTHER Well, gentlemen, I have nothing more to tell him *(pointing to* NTOW*)*. He can go ahead enjoying life – "God humbles him who exalts himself, and exalts him who humbles himself!" Goodbye *(He exits)*.

GYIMA Well, Master, I –

NTOW What is it?

GYIMA Thus a coal pot –

NTOW Are you off your head?

GYIMA Well, your brother-in-law has been speaking to you in proverbs, so why can't I?

NTOW Speaking to whom in proverbs?

GYIMA To you.

NTOW You are going crazy?

GYIMA Not at all!

NTOW Now look! Get out of my way and let me have enough peace of mind to sing.

(Singing joyfully)

I said I should expect you *(Indicating* DONKO *and* YAA ASANTEWA *who have just entered)* at five o'clock,
I said come when it's five o'clock –
This was an agreement with my lovers,
That they should come when it's five o'clock.
And here they are!

DONKO *(Taking over the singing)*

My darling, my darling, Yaw Ntow,
I cannot adequately express my gratitude to you for your kindness.

It's my kinsman who bewitched me and made me keep indoors.

By dear Mary, when shall I expect you?

(Continuing)

I bring you greetings from my people.

NTOW   I accept their greetings sincerely. How did you find your visit?

DONKO   Well, everything went all right during the visit. But our landlord refused to allow us to bring our things because we have not paid our month's rent.

NTOW   Eh! What does he mean?

DONKO   Well, it's a fact!

NTOW   Don't mind him. How much rent do you owe him?

DONKO   We owe him four pounds.

NTOW   Oh! Just four pounds? A minute, please. Look, Gyima, go to my room and look in my drawer. You will find a purse in it. Bring it to me and let me give something to these two ladies.

GYIMA   Why? What is in the purse in the drawer?

NTOW   Hmmm!

GYIMA   You are saying hmm, do you have a drawer? Wasn't all the furniture bought by somebody else?

(NTOW shouts at him and GYIMA runs from the room)

DONKO   My darling, have you sent –

NTOW   Oh, yes, I have sent him!

DONKO   Then let us make ourselves happy.

(NTOW and DONKO sing and dance)

Come oh! come oh! come:/:
Come oh! come oh! come,
Come and entertain me.
My sweet handsome darling,
My darling, a king of beauty,
Your absence makes me sleepless,
Your absence makes me sleepless,
Your neck is one of your chief beauties –
I feel unwell during your absence.
A king of beauty, come and entertain me.

GYIMA *(Interrupting with shouting)*   My goodness! Oh my! *(He repeats this three times)* By Jove! –

NTOW   Hei! What's wrong?

GYIMA *(Continues shouting)*   A bad company ruins an innocent person! Oh, my! I am bewildered.

DONKO   Look! What's wrong? What's wrong?

NTOW   Look! What's the matter with you?

GYIMA *(Reproachfully)*   Master, eh master!

NTOW   Yes?

GYIMA   Your wife Auntie Awura Akua...

NTOW *(Embarrassed)*   Hei!

GYIMA *(Slowly)*   Your wife Auntie Awura Akua...

NTOW   Whose wife?

GYIMA *(Sobering down)*   Your wife Auntie Awura Akua! *(He exits)*

NTOW   You are crazy.

DONKO   Come! Come! Come! Father Yaw Ntow. Why have you kept silent about the fact that you have a wife?

NTOW   Whom do you mean?

DONKO   I mean you, Father Yaw Ntow.

NTOW   You mean me, Yaw Ntow?

DONKO   Didn't you hear your boy telling us so?

NTOW *(Very emphatically)*   I don't have any wife at all.

DONKO   You better not say so if you have a wife.

NTOW *(Pointing at GYIMA)*   He is talking about a woman who lives behind this house of mine.

DONKO   Father Yaw Ntow, do you mean you don't have a wife?

NTOW   Yes. That's what I mean.

DONKO   If you really have a wife, don't be afraid nor feel shy, just summon up courage and tell me. Otherwise, if one of these days a woman finds me here, then I shall prove to her that I am a Fante too.

NTOW   That's right.

DONKO   I mean it, I shall prove to that woman that I am also a woman.

NTOW   Yes, you are a woman, and I am also a man, is that not so?

DONKO   *(Suspiciously)*   That's right! But money determines these things! *(She intimates that she knows* AWURA AKUA *has given money to* NTOW *to sustain him)*

NTOW   What an idea! Let nobody bother me with anything like that.

DONKO   I am just saying these things because there is a proverb which says that "a banana peel which we leave behind after eating is a reminder of a past incident!"

> *(*GYIMA *enters looking very distressed. Throughout the following scene,* DONKO *watches superciliously from the back)*

GYIMA   Master, Master!

NTOW   What's the matter?

GYIMA   Look, Auntie Awura Akua has been injured in an accident and I want to go to help her.

NTOW   If she has sustained some injuries, was it I who caused the injuries?

GYIMA   *(Forcefully)*   She has had an accident.

NTOW   You are crazy!

GYIMA   *(Very reproachfully)*   Are you telling me now that she isn't your wife? All right, I shall go and fetch her and you will see whether or not she is your wife. But she has been hurt. Your wife has been hurt!

> *(*ALL *exeunt)*

> *(Musical interlude during short intermission)*

> *(Enter* GYIMA *and* AWURA AKUA, *who is limping and is bandaged.* YAW NTOW *stands in the background)*

AKUA   *(Singing)*   Oh, I'm tired of too much traveling —

GYIMA   It's true we are weary from traveling.

AKUA   *(Singing)*

> Oh, my burden is heavy,
> I am wondering how I can get home,

I look to the Almighty for strength
It is he who will guide me.

AKUA *[Seeing* NTOW *who now comes forward]*   Hallo! my darling!

NTOW Who is that?

AKUA I am your wife, Awura Akua.

NTOW You seem to be off your head. Whose wife?

AKUA I am your wife, Awura Akua.

NTOW Are you crazy, who, do I know you? *[He makes a sign disowning her]*

AKUS Ee! don't you know me?

NTOW Who is your darling? – "You bloody fool."

AKUA Oh, darling!

NTOW Now look, when you compare yourself with me, do you think you are fit to be my darling?

> *[They struggle and* AKUA *is obviously in pain]*

GYIMA Oh, my God, where are you? Oh, who will come to our aid? God, where are you? Oh my lord, ee! *[Wailing]*

> *[*YAA *and* DONKO *join* NTOW *against* AKUA*]*

GYIMA *[Wailing loudly]*   Oh God, hurry up, God hurry up, I am in trouble. Oh! Oh! Oh! Auntie don't you worry. Entrust everything to God.

AKUA *[Singing]*

I weep over my sad fate, oh brethren,
Countrymen, I weep over my illness.
I weep over my sad fate,
Countrymen, I weep over my illness.
As a human being, you may cherish your family relations.

GYIMA *[Singing in response]*

Oh pitiful!
When you are ill
Oh pitiful!
Don't count on your family
Oh pitiful!
Wealth is all that goes to make a family

Oh pitiful!
Therefore I always weep over the possibility of a sad fate,
Countrymen, I weep over my own future illness.

GYIMA *[Joining* AWURA AKUA*'s song]*

Auntie, you are much to be pitied for your illness,
Whom did you call during your illness?
Who came to your aid?
It's only the Almighty God, it's only God who will ever help
    you!
I weep over my own sad fate, Oh brethren,
Countrymen, I weep over my own future illnesses,
I pray to God that I don't stay long in my own sick bed
Oh pitiful!
Because I haven't got any savings
Oh pitiful!
Therefore, I always weep over the possibility of a sad fate
Oh Brethren
Countrymen, I weep over my own future illnesses.

GYIMA *(Singing alone)*

She is much to be pitied for her illness
She's been involved in an accident!

(Addressing AKUA*)* Who will nurse you while you are ill?

AKUA I have been deserted by all my family during my illness,
God. I weep over my illness!

GYIMA Oh! God!

BROTHER *(Entering)* Awura Akua!

AKUA Here I am!

BROTHER Oh! I am looking for you. What has caused this, Awura
Akua? *(He looks at her bandages)*

AKUA *(Mourningly)* This is the condition in which I am, Brother.
It is just about three days ago when I felt I should see Pa. You
weren't around when I was leaving and so I left a message
which I hope you received. Pa even decided to accompany me
on my return trip, to discuss one or two things here. When we
were about three miles from home, our lorry had an accident.
When I regained consciousness, I found myself in a house. I
was informed that three young men conveyed me into this

house. I sent for my husband and the message I received from him was the he didn't know me. When I was conveyed here, he started stamping his feet and telling me that he had married two wives.

BROTHER   Aah!

AKUA   Hmm! Look at my miserable condition and it was worse still according to an eyewitnes account. Pa must have been completely torn to pieces during the accident. Alas, I presume he's dead!

BROTHER   *[Horror-struck]*   You mean he is dead! And I didn't even see his face?

AKUA   Yes! Dead, alas!

BROTHER   Even you who have survived for me to see your face, have bandages all over your body! *[He weeps]*

AKUA   Well, brother, I am almost at the point of dying, and I don't have any money. Thieves have stolen all my belongings from my room, and what shall I do at this moment when I am dying? You told me, but I didn't heed your advice.

GYIMA   Oh! Auntie, don't worry, we understand.

BROTHER   Oh! Awura Akua!

GYIMA   Auntie, at the moment, it's God who will be our support! God exists.

AKUA   Oh! I am dying, let somebody hold me! Oh! Hmm!

GYIMA   Oh! Man, it is miserable here! *[He shows* AKUA *some money]* Look, this is the money which you gave me yesterday. It's the money you gave me to buy something to eat. I didn't spend it because I did not know what the future had in store for us or what might happen to us. I shall take it to the doctor and ask him to come and give you medical treatment. You understand?

AKUA   *[Very touched]*   All right, Gyima.

GYIMA   *[Calling aloud]*   Can anybody help? Where is the nearest doctor? *[He exits]*

BROTHER   I told you, Awura Akua!

AKUA   Yes, you told me and I didn't pay any heed to what you said.

167

BROTHER   I said it, but you didn't accept it.

AKUS   Oh! Today it's all over with me. My father and mother are dead. Look at me, look at my condition.

BROTHER and AKUA *(Singing together)*

> My mother and father are dead.
> Brethren, I am in pain, great pain
> *(They repeat several times)*

> *(DONKO enters)*

DONKO *(Suddenly laughing)*   Encore! Ha! Ha! Ha! *(She moves more to the front of the stage)*

GYIMA *(Returning)*   Auntie, the doctor has asked me to take you to him – You understand?

AKUA   All right.

GYIMA   Let us go.

AKUA   Brother, I am leaving. My heart seems to stop beating. Please follow us later. Obtain a loan of money and come to see me, or else I'll die.

BROTHER   Oh, Awura Akua!

AKUA *(Singing)*

> I am pitiable,
> Let somebody come to my aid.
> Oh, Lord God. I am pitiable,
> Let somebody come to my aid.

BROTHER *(Singing at the same time)*

> Let somebody give me a loan to look after my sister,
> Because I am much to be pitied.
> Let somebody come to my aid!

> *(Continuing to sing)*

> It doesn't pay to be kind, to be kind to a human being,
> No matter whether you sell all your property,
> And use the money to save him from trouble,
> In the next day or two when he is safe and free,
> He turns round and says of you "there goes the thief."
> By Jove! Arrest him,
> Oh, my! My goodness! Arrest him!

Oh my! My goodness! Arrest him!
Oh my! My goodness! Arrest him!
Oh my! My goodness! Arrest him!
Oh my! My goodness! Arrest him!

(He continues)

Ntow, you're all talk! You delight in litigation. You will be miserable.

(He sings)

You are all talk, brother-in-law,
You delight in litigation and so you have no respect for anything.
You think you are wise.
You will one of these days "greet a monkey"*
You are all talk,
You are bound to be miserable some day.
Busy body – body Ntow –

DONKO *(Singing)*

If you intend to deal with us, then,
You better buy good clothes for yourself.
Buy new clothes, buy new clothes
Because we hate shoddy clothes.
We hate the shoddy clothes we first saw you wearing!

NTOW and YAA *(Joining in)*

We hate shoddy and poor clothes:/:
If you were a Ghana penny,
I wouldn't use you for my bus fare.
If you were a Ghana sixpence,
I wouldn't use you to buy fanta.

BROTHER *(Singing and pointing to DONKO and YAA)*

Ladies, if you intend to speak to me, then you better go and put on good clothes,
Because I hate shoddy clothes.
Look, the young men who wear good quality clothes, the

---

*Greet a monkey: You will do what human beings don't do, greet an animal because of your excessive wisdom. It is an Akan idiom.

young men who wear gabardine clothes and roam up and down the streets,
Some go to beg for the clothes to wear,
Some buy them and wear them on credit:/:
The young women who wear different kinds of scarves –
Some go to beg for the clothes to wear,
They buy them and wear them on credit:/:
Brethren I can't steal to be laughed at by women,
If I ever buy a gabardine suit on credit,
And I don't get money to pay my rent,
The police may come and arrest me.
While I am being taken away by the police,
It is you, this very woman, a notorious liar,
Who will hide on the way,
And mock me.
She will certainly mock me *(repeating three times)*
Lady! Your father can't manufacture gabardine,
Lady! Your mother too can't manufacture even shoddy clothes,
Gabardine and shoddy clothes are all manufactured by the Europeans:/:
Auntie, if you ladies too intend to speak to me, then
You better wear *kente* cloth:/:
Because I have shoddy clothes,
These shoddy clothes, lady, I hate shoddy clothes:/:

DONKO *(Singing)*

If you insult me, I shall retort insult for insult *(repeats three times)*.

NTOW *(Joining in)*

I shall insult you *(repeats three times)*,
If you insult me I shall retort insult for insult *(repeats four times)*
You look really shabby!

GYIMA *(Responding)*   It's your grandma who looks shabby!

BROTHER *(Singing)*

These women *(pointing to* DONKO *and* YAA*)* consider themselves exceedingly beautiful.
These who are standing behind me, countrymen, deem

themselves more beautiful than all the women gathered here.

These women, brethren, consider themselves exceedingly beautiful.

If you do undress them, you will be surprised to see that their bodies are completely covered with rashes.

DONKO *[Singing]*

I beseech God always to give me patience,

NTOW and YAA *[Joining in]*

May he always give me patience,
May God always give me patience,
Because patience is an exceptional virtue.

BROTHER *[Singing]*

The lady says
God should give her patience, do you hear that?
What does she want God to give her patience for?
Do you want God to give you patience so that you can lead an immoral life? *[repeats three times]*
For you to undertake evil deeds?
Auntie, what do you want God to give you patience for?:/:
What are you going to do with the patience you want from God?
Look, all your friends are married except you,
Some of them have even had their first babies;
Your childbearing seems too much delayed.
Is that why God should give you patience?
What type of life do you want the patience for?
Is that why God should give you patience?
What will you do with the patience you want from God?
May God always give you wisdom,
May he always give you thoughtfulness,
For you to lead a good life, always;
Yes, so that you may at least have one baby.

BROTHER   Yes, but I would like to tell you, Father Ntow, as well as your women, that my sympathies are rather more with them than with you. You now already have a wife and as soon as you met them, you deserted your wife –

NTOW   I have a wife! Who married a wife for me?

171

BROTHER   And the women, too, are pleased to have you following them. They are happy to see you gorgeously dressed in
kente, but they don't know where it came from. They don't
know that! Whatever ill-treatment you meted out to a woman
will be shortly also meted out to you!

GYIMA   There isn't much time left for them to suffer the same
fate.

> *[Throughout the following scene,* GYIMA *listens with a dis-
> dainful expression]*

BROTHER   I have nothing more to say. Ladies and gentlemen, I
should like to beg leave of you so that I can go and see my sister
in the hospital; it is high time I ended this singing and dancing.
My attention is now focused on my sister who is in hospital. I
should rather request your prayers for my sister's speedy
recovery and against anything like death. If we return to find
that Ntow and his women have left for overseas, then my sister
and I, too, will eventually travel overseas to let them know that
we, too, can go there.

> *[He sings]*

Let those who have taken the lead go,
Let the lucky ones go,
I shall travel slowly to my destination.
Look, I shall travel slowly to my destination.
No man knows what fate has in store for another man.
No man knows another man's destiny –
Fortunes come to men in turns,
To some in the morning, to some in the afternoon and to
   others in the night.
When is my turn? I have been left behind by all my mates;
   but need I die on account of that?
No! I shall travel slowly to my destination.

> *[*BROTHER *exits]*

DONKO   Father Yaw Ntow!

NTOW   Yes.

DONKO   Please, I would like to ask you one question. Has your
mind been disturbed by what has been going on?

NTOW   Oh, no! My mind is not in the least disturbed.

DONKO   Don't let anything disturb your peace of mind.

NTOW   That's right.

DONKO   If you have made up your mind to stay with us, that is with Madam Yaa Asantewaa and myself, Donko, then we too are prepared to stay with you through thick and thin, to the end of our lives.

NTOW and DONKO *(Singing)*

> I love you, I'll be with you always,
> My darling handsome young man.
> Your woe is my woe,
> I love you.
> *(They repeat several times)*

DONKO   Father Yaw Ntow, life is really . . .

NTOW and DONKO *(Together)*   What you make of it, "each for himself and God for us all."

DONKO   I could see that our marriage is an established union, so we would like to ask your leave and go to bring all our belongings to this town.

NTOW   All right! All right!

DONKO   Please give us four pounds to go and pay our landlord.

NTOW   All right!

DONKO   So that we can bring all our belongings here.

NTOW   That's right! But I'm now going to tell you that you should accept this two pounds —

DONKO   Oh. But that's not four pounds, is it?

NTOW   Yes, I know it is not enough. You just go to the Ghana Commercial Bank and ask them for any amount of money. You will be given it because I built the bank.

DONKO   You mean the Ghana Commercial Bank?

NTOW   Yes, I built it. You just mention my name, Father Yaw Ntow, to the authorities there and you will be given any amount of money you need. When you get it, use some of it to pay your rent.

DONKO   Do you mean the Commercial Bank situated on the curve?

NTOW   That's right, you even know it already.

DONKO   All right.

NTOW   When you get to the bank, you only have to mention my
name and everything will be all right.

DONKO   Well, then, please give us a check.

NTOW   Oh, no! If I do that it will mean I also have an account
there, that is, I am also a customer.

DONKO   Ah! Is that right?

NTOW   Yes, but you know I built the bank with my own money.
I own it.

DONKO   So you mean we only need to mention your name and —

NTOW   That's what I mean.

DONKO   *(Singing)*

I'll always be with you till death, darling;
I'll always move with you till death, darling.

NTOW   *(Joining in)*

I'll always be with you till death, my darling:/:
My darling, I'll always be with you till death.

(DONKO and YAA ASANTEWAA exeunt)

GYIMA   Master! Master!

NTOW   Who is that? What's the matter?

GYIMA   *(Sardonically)*   In all you have been doing, you seem to be
enjoying yourself as much as you might do on Christmas Day.
Don't you think so?

NTOW   Now, don't bother me with idle talk.

*(Musical interlude. GYIMA sings a song in a Nigerian lan-
guage)*

(DONKO and YAA ASANTEWAA enter)

DONKO   Greetings from our people.

NTOW   Thank you, I welcome their greetings.

DONKO   Oh, darling, when we left this place, we hurriedly hired
a taxi on the street and went straight to the Ghana Commercial
Bank. On arrival there, we went to one of the clerks and men-

tioned your name to him. It may surprise you that he got very annoyed and furious and told us that as the bank wasn't the one you built, he wouldn't give us the money. That's why we have returned.

NTOW Are those people in the bank over there off their heads?

DONKO We didn't get the money.

NTOW *(Shouting)* Didn't you get it?

DONKO No, we didn't!

NTOW Is the taxi you hired still around?

DONKO Yes.

NTOW Hurry up then and let us take it to the place.

DONKO All right!

NTOW *(Quickly but quietly approaching GYIMA)* Please lend me some money.

GYIMA Eh! Why do you want money from me?

NTOW *(Aloud to DONKO)* Look! Check to see if the taxi is still there.

DONKO All right, I'll do that.

GYIMA Eh! Master, are you short of money?

NTOW *(Softly to GYIMA)* Just two pounds. *(Aloud)* The two pounds I am collecting from you, doesn't that –

DONKO *(From the back of the stage)* The taxi is still waiting for you!

NTOW I am coming along. I am ready for us to go.

GYIMA He is coming, he is coming. *(He gives money to NTOW)* Here is it, take it. *(As NTOW stretches his hand to receive it, GYIMA withdraws his hand and says)* He is taking it! Now go and squander it! *(He grins cheekily)*

NTOW Donko!

DONKO Sir, here I am.

NTOW Come! Come! Come here, because I am really annoyed.

DONKO Please, here I am.

NTOW You realize I am quiet?

DONKO   Yes.

NTOW   I presume you heard these people hooting?

DONKO   Yes, I heard them.

NTOW   I am so annoyed *(calming down)* I . . . I told my boy what had happened. I presume you saw me standing here with him?

DONKO   Yes.

NTOW   I told him what had happened and said that I had decided to go with you and collect the money for you. To that my boy said, "Master you are aware that you have a hot temper. If you go, you are most likely to dismiss or fire all the clerks over there and make trouble for them." But I told him that I had to go with you – Therefore, you will have to stay the night here. *(He winks at the audience)* You will have to stay the night here so that I go with you tomorrow.

DONKO   Do you mean I should stay here till tomorrow?

NTOW   Yes.

DONKO   How far is it from here to Accra? Do you want me to stay here until tomorrow?

NTOW   Now look, just listen to what I am telling you –

DONKO   Do you think we do nothing in Takoradi where we live?

NTOW   Now look, I hate a woman who makes a face while speaking to a man. If you continue to do that, I shall refuse to go and collect the money for you. *(Adding firmly)* I am no longer going to collect the money for you.

DONKO   What the hell do you mean, that you are no longer going?

NTOW   I am not going with you; I am not!

DONKO   Don't say you won't go, say you can't get the money. I could see that you don't have any money. I really don't want anybody passing by to hear me talking so that he asks me what's the matter? This is because you and I are not of the same social class. That will cast a slur on me; it will disgrace me. Do you understand? You certainly are not of my class. It is merely because of the unfortunate circumstances in which I find myself, that I am talking in this way before the honorable ladies and gentlemen gathered here. Father Yaw Ntow, henceforth when you meet me in the street and you "feel like greeting me, just pass by and go." I am not a small boy for you to be calling, Donko, Donko. If you ever do that I shall speak to you in real Fante idiom.

NTOW   I should like to tell you that since you came here I have never had any love for you.

DONKO   Shame! Shame on you!

GYIMA *(Wisely)*   Well, master, you will soon learn that these are harlots from Kumasi.

DONKO   Come, come, Father Yaw Ntow. Ntow, tell me what do you think of us? What do you think we are?

NTOW   Oh! Is that it? —

DONKO   I dislike nonsense. The truth is when we went to the bank, we could not get the money. The manager went to the extent of slapping our faces. I don't intend having any long argument with you. At present, I can see that you don't have any money on you.

NTOW   Oh! well. . .

DONKO   You want to deceive us. It is you who have tricked me into staying in this house and made me lose opportunities for making money. The white man says, "time is money." You have wasted too much of my time. As I said, I don't intend arguing with you. I am just taking this cloth of yours to sell so that I can pay the landlord. *(She pulls the cloth from him)*

NTOW   Eh! Wait! Wait!

GYIMA *(Singing)*

This is Uncle who always buys on credit,
That's he! His creditors have come to collect their money!
This is Uncle who always buys things on credit,
That's surely he. His creditors have come to collect their money.

NTOW   Oh, wait a minute! Wait! I never like to be disgraced, I really don't. . . . Ladies and gentlemen *(addressing the audience)*, did you see Awura Akua behave in this way while I was here with her? Even Awura Akua?

DONKO   Ladies and gentlemen *(also addressing the audience)*, any of you who would like to buy this cloth and these shoes should come forward and I'll sell them to him.

177

GYIMA   I will buy them.

DONKO   Would you really like to buy them?

GYIMA   How much do they cost?

DONKO   I shall accept twenty-five pounds for them.

GYIMA   Do you mean the cloth?

DONKO   That's right.

GYIMA   All right, I understand. How about these? *(Pointing to the pair of sandals)*

DONKO   For these, even four pounds will be an acceptable bid.

GYIMA   All right, let not this be a long and troublesome bargaining. I would just like to dance with you before I pay you.

DONKO   You want to dance with me first?

GYIMA   Yes.

DONKO   What kind of dance is it? And why?

GYIMA   Oh, aren't you the person demanding the money?

DONKO   But why?

GYIMA   *(Persuasively)*   Won't you dance?

DONKO   *(Hesitatingly)*   Well, I guess I have no choice. I shall dance. . . . What kind is it to be?

GYIMA   *(Starting to dance)*   Is that right?

DONKO   What type of dance do you mean?

GYIMA   Highlife.

DONKO   Highlife – All right. I will dance with you. *(They dance together, but* GYIMA *dances lewdly till they are both exhausted)*

DONKO   Now tell me, where did you learn all these dances?

GYIMA   You mean these dances?

DONKO   Yes.

GYIMA   In America.

DONKO   Now listen to me. I have done everything you wanted me to do for you. It remains my money. Could you please pay me and let me go?

GYIMA   I am afraid, this type of *kente* cloth is not worn in my

178

home town. So I don't think I can wear it there. Therefore, please take it back. I don't like it. At the moment, I have worn it free of charge. I shan't pay a penny for that. *[He addresses the audience]* Beloved brethren, ladies, lasses, and girls, I should like to ask your permission to go and see Auntie Awura Akua who has sustained serious injuries. If I don't hurry and she dies, then my breakfast will similarly die, too, tomorrow morning. In the light of this, I am begging leave of you to go. Do you understand? Goodbye for now.

DONKO   Take your hat. You have succeeded in fooling me.

GYIMA   Yes, I have fooled you. *[He exits]*

DONKO   Countrymen, I guess I needn't worry. I have realized that my journey to this place has been fruitless. *[She sings]*

> I made this journey to make money.
> If I have been unsuccessful in making money to take to my home town, then, as an orphan, bury me wherever I die.
> Brethren, I am the loser in our life struggle.
> Ladies and gentlemen, I am selling these articles.
> Whoever wants to buy them may do so.
> If I fail to get somebody to buy them, maybe in the future, I can give them to my boyfriend.
> I am miserable today.

> *[DONKO exits and a short while later, GYIMA returns]*

GYIMA   Beloved friends, young women, lads, and lasses. . . . God, Almighty God, I render my sincerest thanks to you. I am happy to announce that by the grace of God, Auntie Awura Akua has fully recovered from the injuries she sustained. She has now put on flesh. Ladies and gentlemen, here is Awura Akua. Clap for her, all of you!

> *[AWURA AKUA, recovered and clad in beautiful clothes, enters with her BROTHER, and a musical interlude occurs as they come onstage. When the music stops, the two sing]*

AKUA *[Singing]*

> I sometimes feel cold;
> I am sometimes chilled to the bone, darling.

BROTHER *[Singing]*

> My darling, come and make me happy;

My beauty, come and make me happy;
My darling, my beautiful darling, come and make me happy.

AKUA   Oh! Gyima.

GYIMA   Auntie!

AKUA   Gyima!

GYIMA   Auntie, Auntie, you are making me feel crazy.

BROTHER Ladies and gentlemen gathered here –

GYIMA   Eh! Man, now you have almost changed to a presbyter.
(He laughs)

BROTHER Ladies and gentlemen here present, those of you who
help me, those of you whose prayers spurred me on to go and
take care of my sister in hospital, I thank you sincerely in the
name of God. As you can see for yourself, my sister didn't die;
she stands right beside me looking radiant. *(He laughs)* I would
like to point out a fact which must be common knowledge to
you all, namely that every man encounters mishaps in life. Just
as one person encounters his, then another person will shortly
do the same.

GYIMA   Eh! Auntie!

AKUA   Gyima!

GYIMA   The song you have been singing is extremely sweet – as
sweet as fried fish.

BROTHER Ladies and gentlemen, you remember my sister told
you that the lorry on which she and other people were traveling
had an accident and that she did not see what happened to our
Pa? She was fortunate in being conveyed to a certain house by
some kind people, as a result of which she is alive today. I am
happy to say that just as in my sister's case, some kind people
also took care of our father. My sister was unconscious at the
time because of her injuries. She did not know what happened.
Somebody has been kind enough to give us a hint that our Pa is
receiving treatment in a certain village. My sister and I have
decided to pay a visit to him to find out his state of health. I am
so happy! Ladies and gentlemen, I am so hale and hearty that if
I had to fight, I would be wonderful. My present strength is
comparable to electric power. I may give somebody a thorough
beating today.

GYIMA   I would like to get a particular type of food to eat.

BROTHER   Awura Akua, let us go so that we return in time.

AKUA   Gyima!

GYIMA   Auntie!

AKUA   Why don't you accompany us on our trip?

GYIMA   All right, Auntie.

AKUA   You have been tremendously kind to me. I don't have adequate words to render my hearty thanks to you. Do you understand?

GYIMA   Am I hearing aright?

AKUA   Yes, you have patience, do you understand?

GYIMA   Does it mean you plan to render thanks to me?

AKUA   Yes, I do, but let us first pay a visit to my father and I shall tell you whatever I have decided when we return. Do you understand?

GYIMA   You may thank me now.

AKUA   Now wait a minute, that is not how we do things.

(OLD MAN enters)

OLD MAN   Eh! Awura Akua.

AKUA   Hallo! Pa! Pa!

GYIMA   Hallo! Papa!

OLD MAN *(Embracing AKUA)*   Hallo! Awura Akua, I am glad to see you!

GYIMA   Hallo! Old man, thanks be to Almighty God! *(He jumps on the back of the OLD MAN)*

BROTHER   Hallo! Papa hallo! Papa!

OLD MAN   Awura Akua, who's this man? Where is he from?

AKUA   Have patience, Papa. The young man who jumped on your back is a houseboy to my husband, Father Yaw Ntow. You remember I told you a lot about this boy? We have just been whiling away our time here. You have just arrived. You tell us about your venture.

OLD MAN   His being your husband's houseboy doesn't give him any right to jump on my back, does it?

181

AKUA   Well, Pa, I suspect he was over-excited on seeing you alive, because we had thought that you were dead – until this evening when we heard that you were being given medical treatment in a certain village. It was excitement and nothing else which made him jump on your back.

OLD MAN   Granted, he was happy and excited, did jumping on my back add anything to his excitement and happiness?

AKUA   Please, Pa, pardon him.

OLD MAN   He knows very well that I am not in perfect health and that I was involved in a lorry accident and I have just recovered from the injuries I sustained. Why did he jump on my back in the way he did?

AKUA   Papa, please, pardon him, pardon him!

OLD MAN   *(Addressing* GYIMA*)*   Do you delight in my death or my safety?

GYIMA   Please forgive me; I won't do it again.

OLD MAN   This boy appears to be a ruffian. He's a rascal – Akua, I don't think I have a lengthy story to tell. We were on a lorry from Accra. We had just passed the Cantonment Road, a bit –

AKUA   That's right!

OLD MAN   – I just didn't see what happened. What I suddenly heard was a terrible crashing noise.

AKUA   Oh, Papa! I also didn't see what happened.

OLD MAN   I found myself at Ayikuma when I regained consciousness. Why there, you may ask! How did I find myself there? I enquired about it – I found that my neck as well as my chest had been bandaged very firmly. I was told that during the accident I fell into a ditch where none of the people on the lorry saw me. I was only lucky that when certain drivers were passing by, they heard me groaning in the ditch.

AKUA   Hm! Oh, God!

OLD MAN   They came to pick me up and when they discovered I had broken ribs and a swollen neck, they took me to Ayikuma and put me in the charge of a traditional healer who is well known for treating such injuries. I was with him when I regained consciousness and then I remembered that I was traveling with you.

AKUA   Papa, did you remember that I was also on the lorry?

OLD MAN   I then asked where you were.

AKUA   Ao!

OLD MAN   And they told me that I was the only person they found in the ditch.

AKUA   Hmm!

OLD MAN   There was nobody who could tell me where you were. When my condition gradually improved, and I finally recovered from the injuries, I decided to come in search of you. I learnt that you were sent to the Military Hospital and so I hurriedly went there, but on my arrival, I was told that you had been discharged and you were here.

AKUA   Yes, I was discharged today.

OLD MAN   And that is why I have rushed to you here.

AKUA   You are welcome, Pa.

OLD MAN   My sufferings were indescribable.

AKUA   Hm! Let us sympathize with each other.

BROTHER   We should render thanks to God. May the Lord bless us! We owe many thanks to God!

GYIMA   Welcome! Welcome!

OLD MAN   Thank you.

GYIMA   Thank you, in my position as a Nigerian houseboy.

OLD MAN   This boy isn't at all good. His rascality is spoiling him.

AKUA   Well. . . . Papa, I also didn't see what happened during the accident. I found myself in a house when I became conscious. When I came to meet my husband here, that young man surprised me by his behavior.

OLD MAN   Did he take good care of you?

AKUA   He did what? Hm – Father Yaw Ntow? I came to find that he had married two women. He had really married two women, Pa!

OLD MAN   Do you mean Father Yaw Ntow whom I met here?

AKUA   Yes.

OLD MAN   Do you mean that stupid and shabbily dressed man

who stood here like a dunce? That man whom you spent money to help has married two women?

AKUA   He has married two women, Pa.

OLD MAN   Tell me what happened.

AKUA   He told me in front of them that he had never in his life known me.

OLD MAN   Did he say he didn't know you?

AKUA   He even kicked me with his foot. He was helped in this by his wives – I can't describe what they did to me.

OLD MAN   Did they treat you, an injured person, in that way?

AKUA   Yes, Papa!

OLD MAN   Tell me!

AKUA   Thus I decided to go home to collect some money for treatment, only to find that thieves had broken my door, entered the room, and stolen all my things, together with all my money. Therefore, to cut a long story short, that man didn't help me when I needed his help. He divorced me and I now don't know where he is.

OLD MAN   Awura Akua, I told you that very day I met that man here, I detected that he was a bad man. I told you that he had failed in life so you shouldn't follow him and move about with him. Your reply to this piece of advice was that he was the only man you loved.

AKUA   Well, what could I do?

OLD MAN   You see what he has done to you? But where is he himself? Where is Yaw Ntow himself?

AKUA   Your guess is as good as mine; I just don't know where he is. Please ask his boy, he may know.

OLD MAN   *(Asking* GYIMA*)*   Look, where is your master?

GYIMA   You want my master, just a second. *(He calls* NTOW *from the back of the stage.* NTOW *appears disguised as a photographer)* Eh! So you have had to turn yourself into a photrographer today.

BROTHER   *(Surprised)*   Awura Akua! Is this not Yaw Ntow?

GYIMA   Oh, no! He isn't Yaw Ntow today. He is Joe Tetteh Number Two.*

OLD MAN   Awura Akua, do you tell me you bought clothes and a *kente* from him and in addition gave him some money to spend while at work?

AKUA   Papa, I don't think it proper to say anything. I'd rather he speak for himself if only he is prepared to speak the truth.

OLD MAN   The clothes and the cloth she bought for you –

NTOW   Yes, it's true she bought clothes for me. After that I came in search of money, and she gave me about four pounds. While the money was on me, I met two young women who were in dire need of money, so I gave them the money. They came again to tell me that they needed money to pay their rent. But having then exhausted all my money, I stripped off the *kente* cloth and gave it to them to go and pay their rent.

AKUA   Oh my!

OLD MAN   Do you expect a man with any intelligence to behave in the way you did? You were hard up with not even a cent on you and a woman squeezed her purse for money to buy clothes and a cloth for you; on top of that, you had a job and you needed four pounds for it, and she gave you that amount too. How come that you met some young women who were in need of money so that you gave them the money given you by Awura Akua?

NTOW   Ah, what?

OLD MAN   And when they told you that they had no money to pay their rent too, you stripped off the cloth –

NTOW   The *kente* cloth which she bought.

OLD MAN   That was the cloth you gave them to go and sell for four pounds.

NTOW   Yes, I gave it to them to go and sell – I just didn't have any money on me.

OLD MAN   *(Sighing)*   Hmm!

---

*Joe Tetteh is a Ghanaian boxer.

185

AKUA   Good Lord!

OLD MAN   When such a kind wife, who had furthermore sustained injuries during a lorry accident, came to you, you had the nerve to disown her, and you and your women kicked her wounds with your feet?

NTOW   Oh no! We didn't do that!

AKUA   Pa, he surprises me. *(Addressing* NTOW*)* Now tell the truth, didn't you kick me with your feet?

OLD MAN   Are you denying that you kicked her wounds with your feet?

> *(*OLD MAN *moves towards* NTOW *who dodges; he and* NTOW *indulge in hide and seek)*

OLD MAN   *(Finally remarking)*   I am very much annoyed!

BROTHER   Well, old man, people interpret things in their own way. In my youthful opinion, you should get Awura Akua to ask Ntow where he left the *kente* cloth so that he goes to redeem it with money and brings it to wear. Otherwise, in the near future it may be alleged that when Awura Akua sustained injuries in a lorry accident, Ntow raised a loan to give her medical treatment and when she recovered the creditor asked for his money which Ntow failed to pay back and his cloth was confiscated. People will wrongly interpret the incident in that way. Please let us redeem the cloth for him. Let us end the matter that way and let Ntow take his troubles away. This is my suggestion.

OLD MAN   Do you mean we should do that on top of all the maltreatment he meted out to Awura Akua? You suggest Awura Akua, after such maltreatment, should give money to redeem the cloth for Ntow?

BROTHER   Old man, it doesn't matter at all, does it? That's my opinion.

OLD MAN   I can see that you have no sympathies for Akua at all.

BROTHER   I say it doesn't matter. He maltreated me badly too, but I say it doesn't matter.

OLD MAN   After all that I have been saying —

BROTHER   It doesn't matter, old man. Let her redeem the cloth for him.

(NTOW is pleased and so he bluffs)

OLD MAN   You do not consider what I have been saying – Do you really insist that she should redeem the cloth for him?

BROTHER   Old man, I say it doesn't matter.

OLD MAN   If I had my way, I wouldn't do it. *(He hands a cloth to NTOW who was dressed only in pants)* Come for it, come . . . come . . . come for it. *(NTOW is ashamed and hesitates; however, he goes for it)*

BROTHER   Old man, don't be annoyed. It's you, old man, who gave a proverb which says "When a baby discharges urine on the thigh of his father or mother, they don't cut the thigh away, they clean it." In the same way, if Ntow has dirtied his father's thigh, let us clean it.

OLD MAN   At the moment I am so annoyed that if this boy *(indicating NTOW)* remains in this house or town, I may very soon find myself committing murder. For that reason, I don't want to see him around any more. Awura Akua!

AKUA   Yes, Pa.

OLD MAN   Go and bring five pounds to redeem the *kente* cloth for him; but we should after that see him off to his town. I don't want him to stay in this town, lest the youth here emulate his bad character. Fetch the money to redeem the cloth for him so that we "dispatch" him to his town; yes, let's get rid of him, get rid of him – I don't want to entertain him here anymore.

AKUA   Well – where is the young man?

GYIMA   Eh! Which young man? Do you mean my master. He has been running like a soldier's motorcycle.

(NTOW is trying to slink away unnoticed)

AKUA   But where can we find the clothes?

NTOW   They are with a certain woman.

AKUA   Who knows where the woman lives?

NTOW   Gyima knows the place.

AKUA   Hm. Ha! Ha! *(laughing)* How much money is needed to redeem the things?

NTOW   Five pounds.

AKUA   How much?

187

NTOW   Five pounds.

AKUA   Now tell me, will you wear the cloth again if I redeem it
for you?

NTOW   You want to know whether I shall wear it?

AKUA   Will you wear it?

NTOW   Yes.

OLD MAN   Nonsense! *(He moves towards* NTOW, *who dodges)*

AKUA   I don't want to drag out this business. A father needs to be
obeyed by his child. If a person disobeys his father, he may run
into trouble. I have already disobeyed my Pa once and seen the
consequences. I don't know what the consequences will be if I
disobey him the second time. *(Addressing* NTOW*)* So, I shall
redeem the cloth for you and when I have done that, then I
shall tell you whatever I have in mind. Do you understand?

GYIMA   Shall I go to redeem it?

AKUA   Yes. You say you know the place, don't you? *(*GYIMA *nods
and exits)*

OLD MAN   The presence of this boy *(pointing to* NTOW*)* annoys me;
I become annoyed as soon as I see him. There will be trouble if I
don't take care.

(Musical interlude)

*(*GYIMA *returns with a cloth and a pair of sandals.* NTOW *takes
them and dresses)*

OLD MAN   It's surprising – this boy has no shame. If he were a real
man, he would be so ashamed of himself that he would be
unable to wear the cloth. But as for this fellow, he has lost all
shame. Look – look, he is bluffing on top of it, look. . . . Oh
God, please give me patience; otherwise I may become violent.
I am sorry about this. God, please cool my temper for me to
Ntow. You are not ashamed of anything. When he gave the
cloth to you, you obviously enjoyed putting it on! *(Moralizing)*
You should realize that there are few really successful marriages. A really true marriage is one in which the man has seen
the woman's people and the relatives of the man too have
known the woman. You should not regard it as a true marriage
when you merely meet a woman who may have left her home-
town and be wandering about, and then you bring her to your

home as a wife. In such a case, you don't know her home nor her relatives; you may deceive yourself that you have had her "cheap." In this world, things acquired cheaply lead to death. When you stay with such a "cheap" wife for whom you have performed no marriage rites, such as the payment of the bride-price and she happens to die in your house, who will be the relative whom you will tell about her death? To which house will you take the dead body? Or into what town will you take it? You will thus have the dead body of somebody's relative left on your hands. Similarly, if a woman lives with a man as a husband and she does not know any relations of the man and she doesn't bother to know any, the man happens to die, how can she then face the man's relatives? Will she be in a position to perform the customary funeral rites incumbent on a widow? The woman, because of her inability to enter the house, may have to resort to wandering outside the dead man's house and have to perform private funeral rites for a friend, instead of a husband. All this will be bad. Therefore, a marriage contracted during a visit is a blasphemy. *[Addressing* NTOW*]* Had it not been for the fact that you are married to my daughter, and your name is associated with hers, I wouldn't give you back this *kente* cloth. It is just because the marriage was properly contracted at home, that's why I am doing this.

AKUA   Well – Papa – please, I'd like to say a word. Can I?

OLD MAN   Yes, go ahead.

AKUA   Eh – Father Yaw Ntow, I am happy my father is here as well as my brother. Your own boy Gyima is also here. I wanted to help you out of your difficulties, but you don't seem to like my help. I can see that you are a beast in human form. I say this without any apologies. I had hoped that if in the near future my father were to die, which God forbid, and I were left with my brother, I could take you to be my father, my husband, my relative and my everything. All my father's wealth would have been yours.

OLD MAN   The Devil follows him.

AKUA   I can see that you like this single *kente* cloth. This single pair of sandals fits you well. Therefore, henceforth, don't regard me as your wife. I shall also not regard you as my husband any longer. Maybe if you get the chance, you will kill me.

189

Let this be the end of our marriage. My only worry is that you may curse me and tarnish my reputation and therefore take this pound for your lorry fare. Don't tarnish my reputation when you go away. When you are in your house and you are eating, you will remember me. Goodbye! We meet some day!

OLD MAN   Take the money.

GYIMA   Take it. I shall stay with Auntie Awura Akua. I know a good family when I see one!

[NTOW *exits, looking very downcast*]

OLD MAN, BROTHER, AKUA, GYIMA   [*Singing together*]

Safe journey, my dear, safe journey:/:
May the Lord guide and guard you in your journey;
My dear, safe journey.
May the Lord guide and guard you in your journey.
My dear, safe journey.

[*Series of songs follows*]

THE END

DATE DUE

Mindal			
MAR 3 0 2006			
	261-2500		Printed in USA